A PENGUIN MYSTERY

THE MADMAN OF BERGERAC

One of the most significant figures in twentieth-century European literature, GEORGES JOSEPH CHRISTIAN SIMENON was born on February 12, 1903, in Liège, Belgium. He began work as a reporter for a local newspaper at the age of sixteen, and at nineteen moved to Paris to embark on a career as a novelist. According to Simenon, the character Jules Maigret came to him one afternoon in a café in the small Dutch port of Delfzijl as he wrestled with writing a different sort of detective story. By noon the following day, he claimed, he had completed the first chapter of *Pietr-le-Letton*, *The Strange Case of Peter the Lett*. The pipe-smoking Commissaire Maigret would go on to feature in seventy-five novels and twenty-eight stories, with estimated international sales to date of 850 million copies. His books have been translated into more than fifty languages.

The dark realism of Simenon's fiction has lent itself naturally to film adaptation, with more than five hundred hours of television drama and sixty motion pictures produced throughout the world. A dazzling array of directors have tackled Simenon on screen, including Jean Renoir, Marcel Carné, Claude Chabrol, and Bertrand Tavernier. Maigret has been portrayed on film by Jean Gabin, Charles Laughton, and Pierre Renoir; and on television by Bruno Cremer, Rupert Davies, and, most recently, Michael Gambon.

Simenon died in 1989 in Lausanne, Switzerland, where he had lived for the latter part of his life.

For Nobel Laureate André Gide, Simenon was "perhaps the greatest novelist" of twentieth-century France. His ardent admirers outside of France have included T. S. Eliot, Henry Miller, and Gabriel García Márquez.

GEORGES SIMENON

THE MADMAN OF BERGERAC

TRANSLATED BY
GEOFFREY SAINSBURY

PENGUIN BOOKS

PENGUIN BOOKS

Published by the Penguin Group

Penguin Group (USA) Inc., 375 Hudson Street, New York, New York 10014, U.S.A.

Penguin Group (Canada), 90 Eglinton Avenue East, Suite 700, Toronto,
Ontario, Canada M4P 2Y3 (a division of Pearson Penguin Canada Inc.)

Penguin Books Ltd, 80 Strand, London WC2R 0RL, England

Penguin Ireland, 25 St Stephen's Green, Dublin 2, Ireland (a division of Penguin Books Ltd)

Penguin Group (Australia), 250 Camberwell Road, Camberwell,
Victoria 3124, Australia (a division of Pearson Australia Group Pty Ltd)

Penguin Books India Pvt Ltd, 11 Community Centre,
Panchsheel Park, New Delhi – 110 017, India

Penguin Group (NZ), 67 Apollo Drive, Mairangi Bay,
Auckland 1311, New Zealand (a division of Pearson New Zealand Ltd)

Penguin Books (South Africa) (Pty) Ltd, 24 Sturdee Avenue,
Rosebank, Johannesburg 2196, South Africa

Penguin Books Ltd, Registered Offices:
80 Strand, London WC2R 0RL, England

First published as *Le Fou de Bergerac* 1932
This translation first published in Penguin Books as part
of the omnibus *Maigret Travels South* 1952
Reissued with revisions and a new introduction in Penguin Classics 2003
Published in Penguin Books 2007

1 3 5 7 9 10 8 6 4 2

Le Fou de Bergerac copyright © 1932. Georges Simenon Limited, a Chorion company.
Translation copyright © 1940, 1952, 2003. Georges Simenon Limited, a Chorion company.
All rights reserved

LIBRARY OF CONGRESS CATALOGING IN PUBLICATION DATA
Simenon, Georges, 1903–1989.
[Fou de Bergerac. English]
The madman of Bergerac / Georges Simenon ; translated by Geoffrey Sainsbury.
p.   cm.
"A Penguin mystery"—
ISBN 978-0-14-311196-2
I. Maigret, Jules (Fictitious character)—Fiction.   2. Paris (France)—Fiction.
I. Sainsbury, Geoffrey.   II. Title.
PQ2637.I53F613   2007
843'.912—dc22   2007000490

Printed in the United States of America

CONTENTS

THE RESTLESS TRAVELER

It all came about by the merest chance. The day before, Maigret hadn't even known he was going on a journey, although it was just the time of year when he had usually had enough of Paris. A month of March spiced with a foretaste of spring. The sun bright, eager, almost warm.

Madame Maigret was spending a fortnight in Alsace with her sister, who was expecting a baby.

But the post this Tuesday morning brought the inspector a letter from an old friend who had retired two years previously from the Police Judiciaire to settle down to country life in the Dordogne.

> And don't forget: if ever a good wind should blow you into this part of the world, I count on you to spend a few days under my roof. My old servant is never so happy as when there's a guest to be made a fuss of . . . The salmon fishing has begun . . .

It was a detail that set Maigret dreaming. The notepaper had a letterhead: the outline of a little manor house, flanked by two round towers. Below this, the words:

LA RIBAUDIERE
NEAR VILLEFRANCHE-EN-DORDOGNE

At twelve Madame Maigret rang up from Alsace to say they were hoping the child would arrive sometime during the night.

"It's just like summer," she added, "and the fruit trees are in blossom . . ."

Yes, it was the merest chance. A little later Maigret was in his chief's room, chatting, when the latter said:

"By the way, did you ever get down to Bordeaux to clear up that matter we were discussing the other day?"

It was a matter of no great importance and of no urgency whatever: Maigret just needed to go down to Bordeaux to look through the municipal records.

Bordeaux . . . Dordogne. A simple association of ideas.

Maigret stared at the ray of sunshine that shone on to the glass ball that the director of the Police Judiciaire used as a paperweight.

"It's not a bad idea," he said. "I've nothing on at the moment."

———

Later that afternoon, armed with a first-class ticket, he got on the train to Villefranche at the Gare d'Orsay. The guard told him he had to change at Libourne.

"Unless you're in the sleeping car—that gets recoupled."

Maigret thought no more about it, looked through two or three newspapers, and then made his way to the dining car, where he lingered over his coffee till nearly ten o'clock.

When he returned to his carriage he found the curtains drawn and the light dimmed. An elderly couple had taken over the two seats.

An attendant passed along the corridor.

"Is there a couchette free?"

"There's nothing first class. But I think there's one in second. If you don't mind . . ."

"Not in the slightest."

And Maigret took his bag down from the rack and followed the man through the corridors, where the latter peeped through door after door till he found a compartment in which only the upper couchette was occupied.

Here too the curtains were drawn, and only the dim light was burning.

"Shall I switch on the light?"

"No, thanks."

The air inside was hot and clammy. From somewhere or other came a faint hiss as if one of the joints of the radiator pipes was leaking. The man in the upper couchette could be heard breathing heavily and tossing about.

The inspector quietly took off his shoes, jacket, and waistcoat, and lay down. His head was in a thin draft.

He couldn't tell where it came from, but by balancing his bowler over one side of his face he was able to ward it off.

Did he fall asleep? Hardly. But at any rate he dozed. Perhaps an hour. Perhaps two. Or it could have been even longer. But however that might be, he never completely lost consciousness.

And in this semiconsciousness the dominant sensation was discomfort. Was it the heat? Or was it the draft, which succeeded after all in getting round the bowler?

They were bad enough, but what really bothered him was the restlessness of the man above.

He couldn't keep still for a minute, nor even for a fraction of a minute. And he was right above Maigret's head. Every time he moved he made a racket. Besides, the man's breathing was irregular as though he was feverish.

At last Maigret could stand it no longer. He went out and started pacing up and down the corridor. There, however, it was too cold.

Back again in the carriage, another spell of troubled somnolence, writhing with sensations and ideas. They were cut off from the rest of the world. The atmosphere was like one in a nightmare.

The man above—had he not leaned over the side of the upper couchette and peered into the shadow in which Maigret lay? Certainly he was never a moment still. Maigret, on the contrary, lay still as a corpse. The half-bottle of claret he had drunk at dinner and the two brandies he had had after it lay heavy on his stomach.

The night dragged slowly on. Now and again the train stopped. There would be voices on the platform, steps in the corridor, the slamming of doors. And each time it seemed as though they were never going to start again.

Was the man weeping? There were moments when his breathing stopped. Then a snuffle. He would turn over and blow his nose.

Maigret regretted his first-class carriage. Why hadn't he stayed there in spite of the elderly couple? He could easily have asked one of them to move.

He dozed, woke, dozed, woke again, until finally he could contain himself no longer. He coughed to clear his throat.

"Excuse me, monsieur, but would you please try to keep still?"

Having said that, he felt more uncomfortable than ever, for his voice had been much gruffer than he had intended. And, after all, the man might be ill . . .

There was no answer. No response whatever, except that the movements overhead ceased. The man must be making a frantic effort not to budge an inch. Then it suddenly occurred to Maigret that it might not be a man after all. Suppose it was a woman? He had never had a real view of the person above him, squeezed in between the bunk bed and the ceiling.

And the heat, which was rising, must be fearful up

there. Maigret tried to turn it half off, but the lever was jammed. It was three o'clock.

"I really must get to sleep."

But he wasn't in the least sleepy now. In fact, he felt almost as jumpy as his traveling companion. He listened intently.

"There we are! He's starting again."

He tried to take no notice, forced himself to breathe regularly, counted up to a hundred and then began again.

There was no doubt about it now—the man was weeping. Probably someone who had been to Paris for a funeral. Or the contrary: some poor devil who worked in Paris, who had received a sudden call to his native town. His mother ill, or perhaps dead. Or it might be his wife. Maigret was sorry he had spoken so roughly. There might even be a coffin in a special wagon attached to the train. Why not? . . .

And then there was his sister-in-law in Alsace . . . She might at any moment be giving birth to her third baby. Her third baby in four years!

Maigret slept.

The train stopped, then went on . . . It raced over a steel bridge, making an infernal din. He opened his eyes abruptly.

The first thing he saw was a pair of legs that dangled from the upper berth. He lay still, watching them. The man was sitting, leaning forward, painstakingly lacing up his boots. In spite of the dimness of the light, Maigret noticed that the boots were of patent leather. The socks, on the other hand, were of thick gray wool, the sort of socks that are generally hand knitted.

The man stopped what he was doing. Was he listening? Had he noticed a change in Maigret's breathing?

Maigret started counting again. But there was no question of his going to sleep now. He was fascinated by the hands that once more went on cautiously lacing up the boots. They trembled. In fact, they shook so much that when the man tried to tie a bow he had to make four shots at it.

They ran through a little station. Lights flicked past, showing faintly through the curtains.

The stranger's feet felt for the little ladder and he started to come down. It was quite ridiculous. He could just climb down normally. Was he scared of being ticked off again?

His foot flailed around, seeking the ladder. He looked like he was about to fall. He turned his back to the inspector.

He went out, forgetting to shut the door behind him, and headed off down the corridor.

If it hadn't been for that open door, Maigret would have turned over with a sigh of relief and gone to sleep at last. But he had to rouse himself to shut it.

As he did so he looked out.

He just had time to slip on his jacket, not bothering about the waistcoat.

He had seen the man open the door at the end of the

corridor. And it was certainly no accident: the train was slowing down.

They were going through a wood. The clouds overhead were lit up by an invisible moon. The brakes went on. A minute or two before, they had been doing eighty kilometers an hour. They had come down to thirty, or even less, when suddenly the man disappeared.

He jumped well clear of the train and rolled down the railway embankment. Maigret did not stop to think what he was about. He simply made a dash for the door. The train had slowed down even more—there was no danger.

He jumped out into the night, landed on his side. He rolled over three times and came to rest next to a barbed-wire fence.

The train rattled on, the red glow from the engine fading away in the distance.

Maigret picked himself up, a little shaken, but with nothing sprained or broken. The other man's fall must have been worse, for he was only now beginning to get to his feet, slowly and painfully, about fifty meters further back.

It was an absurd situation. Ruefully, the inspector wondered what had possessed him to throw himself out into the night like that, leaving his luggage to complete the journey to Villefranche-en-Dordogne. He hadn't even the faintest notion where he was.

Apart from the railway embankment, he could only see trees, except in one place where there was a pale streak of road.

Why didn't the man move? He had risen no farther than to his knees. Was he really hurt? Or had he seen Maigret?

"Hey, you over there," called out the latter, feeling for his revolver.

He had hardly grasped it, however, when he saw a flash. He felt a stab in his shoulder even before he heard the bang.

It was all over in a fraction of a second. The man was on his feet now, and running. Maigret saw him cross the strip of road and disappear into the darkness beyond.

The inspector swore. His eyes were wet, not with pain, but with surprise, anger, confusion. It had happened so quickly. And now he was in a thoroughly sorry plight.

The revolver fell from his hand. He stooped to pick it up, and swore again because his shoulder hurt.

As a matter of fact it was not so much pain as a horrid feeling of blood flowing abundantly, welling out with every pulse.

He stood there at a loss, not daring to run or even to move, no longer bothering about picking up his gun. His temples were moist, and it was difficult to swallow. When he put his hand to his shoulder, it was, as he expected, instantly sticky with blood. He felt for the exact position of the wound and pressed it to stay the bleeding.

Half stunned as he was, he was conscious of the train stopping at some distance, perhaps as much as a kilometer away. He listened hard with a feeling of anguish.

Why should he mind whether it started or not? He simply couldn't help it—he longed for it to start. The empty silence was like a frightening void.

At last! Thank God! The puffing and rumbling began again. Turning toward it, he could just make out the faint red glow moving behind the treetops.

Then nothing. Silence once more. Only Maigret. There all by himself, holding his shoulder with his right hand. Yes, it was the left shoulder that was wounded. He tried to move the arm, but it was too heavy: he could only raise it a few inches.

Not a sound from the wood. Was the man already out of earshot? Or was he lying low among the bushes? Waiting perhaps to finish Maigret off as soon as he reached the road?

"You fool! . . . You fool! . . ."

Maigret cursed himself, feeling utterly forlorn. What on earth had made him think of jumping out of the train? At dawn, his friend Leduc would be waiting for him at the station. There'd be salmon for lunch . . .

He started to walk, dragging his feet, stopping every few meters, then staggering on again. All he could see was that white strip of road, dusty as in midsummer.

He was still bleeding. Not so much as at first, because he stopped most of the flow with his hand. But his hand was sticky with the drying blood.

You wouldn't have thought he'd already been wounded three times in the course of his career. He would have suffered any downright pain rather than feel his blood oozing away like that. He felt as bad about it as if he was being wheeled into an operating theater.

And, after all, it would be pretty stupid, wouldn't it? To die all alone on that dusty road in the middle of the night! Not even knowing where he was! And with his luggage continuing the journey without him.

Was the man there behind the bushes? Never mind! Let him shoot! Maigret plodded on, leaning forward, his head swimming. He came to a milestone, but most of it was in shadow. All he could read by the moonlight was 3 km. 5.

What would it be at three and a half kilometers? What town? Or perhaps a village? A cow mooed ahead. The sky was a little paler. So that was where the day would soon be dawning. He must be walking eastwards.

His traveling companion did not seem to be there. Or, if he was, he must have abandoned the idea of finishing Maigret off. The latter thought he could hold out for a few minutes more. Determined to make the best of them, he walked on, marching in time like a soldier, counting his steps to prevent himself thinking.

That cow must belong to a farm, and farmers were early risers. So there was a chance of finding somebody about.

His shirt was all wet. The blood was trickling right down to his waist, under his belt . . .

Was that a light between the trees? Or was he becoming delirious? . . .

"If I lose a liter of blood . . ." he thought.

Yes, it was a light. Only, he had to cross a ploughed field to reach it. It was heavy going. He could hardly make it. He bumped into an abandoned tractor . . .

"Hallo! . . . Anyone there? . . . Quickly! . . ."

In that "quickly" was a despairing note. He was leaning against the tractor now . . . Slipping . . . Sitting on the ground . . . He heard a door open, saw another light—a lantern . . . Someone holding it up . . .

"Quickly! . . ."

A man was approaching. Would he be able to stop the blood? Perhaps he wouldn't think of it. Maigret's hand was losing its grip. His arm fell limply by his side.

"One, two . . . one, two . . ."

With each pulse the blood oozed from the wound.

———

Confused images with blanks of unconsciousness between them. Tortuous images with the oppressive quality of a nightmare.

A rhythm . . . the steps of a horse . . . straw under his head . . . trees going by . . .

That at any rate was understandable. He was lying on straw in some kind of a cart. It was broad daylight, and they were going slowly along a road bordered by plane trees.

Maigret lay still, with his eyes open. Within his field of vision was a man who strolled along waving a whip.

Nightmares again . . . He had not had a good look at

the man in the train. All he had seen was his outline, the patent-leather boots and the thick grey socks.

So what made him think this peasant was the man from the train? The face he saw was lined and weather-beaten. A long grey mustache. Thick eyebrows. Pale blue eyes that looked straight ahead without so much as a glance at him.

Where were they? . . . Where were they going? . . .

Moving a hand, the inspector was conscious of something strange pressing on his chest. Of course! Bandages . . . Then one idea ran into another and all was confusion again. A ray of sunshine struck his face, making him blink.

Presently there were houses. Houses with white fronts. A wide street bathed in bright light . . . Steps behind the cart. People following . . . And voices . . . But the words were only a jumble . . . The bumping of the cart over the cobbles hurt . . .

The bumping had stopped. He was floating in the air, rocked on something soft, then gliding along with unaccustomed smoothness.

They were wheeling him on a stretcher. In front was a man in a white coat. Gates were shut. Noise of a crowd fading away . . . Someone came running.

"Take him straight into the theater."

Maigret didn't move his head. He didn't think. He just lay looking at whatever passed before his eyes.

They were out of doors again now, going through a garden. A number of small buildings, very clean, built of white brick. People in grey, all dressed alike, sitting on seats. Some had bandaged heads or arms in slings . . . Nurses going to and fro.

He was thinking now, or trying to, groping for a word that kept on eluding him. There it was—hospital!

Where was that peasant who was so like the man in the train? . . . Ow! . . . They were carrying him up-stairs . . . It hurt . . .

When Maigret woke next, it was to see a man wash-ing his hands, at the same time looking gravely at him.

It gave him quite a shock. This man had a little goatee and thick eyebrows. Did he look like the peas-ant? Perhaps. Perhaps not. But he certainly looked like the man in the train.

Maigret opened his mouth, but no words came. The man with the goatee gave orders quietly:

"Put him in Number 3 . . . Better keep him isolated on account of the police."

What? On account of the police? What was the fel-low talking about?

He was wheeled away by people dressed in white. Back through the garden. The sun—he had never seen such a sun before. Bright, jubilant, blazing into every corner.

They put him to bed. The walls were white. It was almost as hot there as in the train . . . Somewhere a voice saying:

"It's the inspector who wants to know . . ."

The inspector? That must mean him . . . But he

hadn't asked anything . . . How absurd it all was! Particularly this business of the peasant, who looked like the doctor, who looked like the man in the train . . .

Had the man in the train a beard or a mustache? Or neither? Were his eyebrows thick?

"Force his mouth open . . . Right! . . . That'll do."

It was the doctor pouring something down his throat . . . Of course! To finish him off. To poison him! . . .

———

Toward evening, when Maigret came to his senses again, the nurse who was watching by his bedside went to the door. Outside, five men were waiting in the corridor. They were: the public prosecutor of Bergerac, the examining magistrate and his clerk, an inspector, and a police pathologist.

"You can come in now, but the doctor says he's not to be tired. By the look in his eyes, I shouldn't be at all surprised if he's mad."

The five men nodded and exchanged glances.

2

FIVE DISAPPOINTED MEN

It was like a badly acted melodrama. The nurse, after a final glance at Maigret, smiled at the five men as she withdrew. A smile which meant:

"I'll leave him to you."

And the five men took possession of the room. They all smiled too, each in his own peculiar way. But all the smiles were equally menacing—so much so that they looked put on for a special purpose. You might have thought they had plotted together to play some practical joke.

"After you, *monsieur le procureur* . . ."

The prosecutor was a very short man with crew-cut hair and a fierce gaze that had no doubt been studiously adopted to fit his profession, and an air of cold disdain that was no less carefully assumed.

He passed the bed with the merest glance at Maigret, then posted himself with his back to the wall not far from the window, where he stood rigidly, hat in hand.

The examining magistrate followed. This time the glance at Maigret was accompanied by an unmistakable sneer. Then the clerk . . . They were now three in line abreast, backs to the wall. Finally, the police pathologist joined them to make a fourth. It was almost as though they had been lined up for an inspection.

That left only the police inspector with the bulging eyes, who appeared to be cast for the role of savior of the righteous.

With a glance at the others he approached the bed and slowly lowered a hand on Maigret's unbandaged shoulder.

"Caught you this time! What?"

It ought to have been extremely funny, but Maigret didn't even smile. On the contrary, he frowned anxiously.

For he was anxious, anxious about himself. The line between dream and reality was already vague enough, and was becoming vaguer by the minute.

Now he found himself the subject of some farcical investigation. The police inspector was obviously thinking himself very smart.

"I must say . . . I'm not sorry to have a look at that mug of yours at last!"

And those four men against the wall, who simply stared and said nothing . . .

Maigret was surprised to hear himself heave a deep sigh. He drew his right hand from under the bedclothes.

"Who were you after last night? A woman? Or a young girl?"

At that, Maigret was overwhelmed—overwhelmed

by the thought of all the talking that would have to be done to put matters straight. It was awful to think of. He was exhausted. His whole body was aching.

"Better . . ." he began with a limp movement of his hand.

They didn't seem to understand, and in a faint voice he repeated:

"Better . . . tomorrow . . ."

He shut his eyes, and in a second all was confusion, until the four men against the wall were all rolled into one person . . . a peasant who was like the doctor . . . who was like the peasant . . . who was like the man in the train . . .

———————

The next morning he was sitting up in bed, or rather propped up by a couple of extra pillows. From that position he watched the nurse as she pottered about in the sunshine, tidying up the room.

She was a fine-looking girl, big and strong, strikingly fair. The glances she kept on throwing at Maigret were at the same time both challenging and nervous.

"Tell me! It was *five* men that came to see me yesterday, wasn't it?"

She answered haughtily:

"You know perfectly well."

"All right . . . Well, tell me what they wanted."

"I've orders not to speak to you. And I'd better warn you that I'll repeat anything you say."

Strangely, Maigret was deriving a subtle pleasure from the situation, much as one tries to hang on to certain dreams in the morning before waking up completely.

The sun was as bright as in picture books of fairy tales. From somewhere outside came the sound of passing cavalry, and suddenly a triumphant blare of trumpets.

At the same moment the nurse passed close to the bed, and Maigret, wishing to attract her attention, plucked at her dress.

She spun round, uttered a piercing shriek, and fled.

It was not till midday that the mists began to lift. The surgeon was busy dressing the wound when the police inspector arrived in a brand-new straw hat and a royal blue tie.

"You haven't had the curiosity to look in my pocket-book?" asked Maigret gently.

"You know very well you haven't got one."

He must have lost it rolling down the railway embankment.

"I see. Everything is clear. Telephone to the Police Judiciaire . . . They'll tell you I'm Divisional Inspector Maigret. Or it might be quicker still to ring up my former colleague, Leduc, who's living at Villefranche . . . But first of all, for the love of God, tell me where I am."

The other was not so easily convinced. There were supercilious smiles, and now and again he nudged the doctor.

The last suspicions were only broken down when

Leduc drove up in his old Ford. Then at last, to many people's disappointment, it had to be admitted that Maigret was really Maigret and not after all the "Madman of Bergerac."

Leduc had the ruddy complexion of a man who leads an easygoing life in the open air. Since leaving the Police Judiciaire he had adopted a meerschaum pipe, whose cherry stem could be seen projecting from his pocket.

"Here's the story in a nutshell. I'm not from Bergerac, but I drive into the market here every Saturday, and I take the opportunity to have a good meal at the Hôtel d' Angleterre . . . Well, it must have been about a month ago that they found a woman's body on the main road out of town. Strangled. But that wasn't all. Having killed her that way, the sadist stuck a long needle right through her heart."

"Who was she?"

"Leontine Moreau. She lived at a farm called Moulin-Neuf. She wasn't robbed."

"Was she . . . ?"

"No, she wasn't tampered with, though she was a good-looking woman of thirty . . . The crime took place at nightfall as she was returning from her sister-in-law's . . . That's the first . . ."

"There were two?"

"Two and a half . . . The second was a girl of sixteen,

the stationmaster's daughter, who had been out for a ride on her bicycle. She was found in the same state."

"At night?"

"She wasn't found till next morning, but she had been killed the evening before . . . Then lastly there was one of the maids of the Hôtel d' Angleterre, who had been to see her brother, a road mender, who was working five or six kilometers out of town. She was on foot. And suddenly someone seized her from behind and threw her down . . . But she's a strapping girl, and she managed to leave a bite in the man's wrist. He swore and made off. She only saw his back as he ran into the bushes."

"Is that all?"

"It's all so far. But the people here are convinced there's a maniac roaming about in the woods. They refuse to believe it could be one of themselves. When the news got around that you'd been found shot, everybody thought you were the murderer and that you'd been after someone again, but had received a wound."

Leduc spoke gravely. He didn't seem to see the comic side of it at all.

"And what's more," he went on, "they won't get the idea out of their heads in a moment."

"Who's in charge of the case?"

"The local people."

"If you don't mind, I think I'll go to sleep now."

He was very weak and had an inexhaustible capacity

for dozing. He didn't really want to sleep, but to doze, to lie in semiconsciousness with his eyes shut. Most of all, he liked to have his head turned toward the window, with the sun shining through his eyelids.

His fancy had now three new characters to play with, to put through their paces like a child drilling his multicolored tin soldiers.

A woman aged thirty from the Moulin-Neuf Farm . . . The stationmaster's daughter . . . The chambermaid of the hotel.

He could remember the wood. Tall dark trees with a white strip of road. And he could imagine the victim lying in the dust while the murderer thrust the long needle through her heart.

It was a weird image. All the more so for being evoked in this spotless private ward, from which the peaceful sounds of the street were clearly audible. He listened to a man, right under his window, who was a full ten minutes trying to get his car started. The surgeon arrived in a smooth, powerful car, which he drove himself. But it was eight o'clock before Maigret saw him.

"Is it serious?"

"It will take some little time to heal. We'll have to keep you in bed for a fortnight."

"Could I be moved to a hotel?"

"Aren't you comfortable here? . . . Of course, if you had someone to nurse you . . ."

"Look here, doctor! Between ourselves, what do you think of this Madman of Bergerac?"

The doctor stood lost in thought so long that Maigret asked again:

"Do you think, like the others, that there's some sort of wild man living in the woods?"

"No."

Of course he didn't. Maigret, in his musings, had recalled several similar cases. Some of them he'd handled himself.

"A man who, in ordinary life, would behave just like you or me—isn't that more likely?"

"Probably," answered the doctor.

"So, as likely as not, he lives in Bergerac, and may easily be a respectable professional man?"

The surgeon looked at him queerly, hesitating. He seemed to have something on his mind.

"Have you any idea?" went on Maigret, watching him closely.

"I've had a great many, one after the other. I pounce on them, and then reject them indignantly . . . But only to come back to them later. If you clear your mind of all prejudices, practically anyone may be suspected of mental derangement."

Maigret laughed.

"So we'd better have the whole town put under observation, from the mayor or even the public prosecutor downward. And of course we'd have to include the whole staff of the hospital."

But the surgeon did not smile.

"Just a moment—keep still!" he said as he probed

the wound with some delicate instrument. "It's a more terrible business than you think."

"What's the population of Bergerac?"

"Sixteen thousand . . . But to my mind everything points to its being someone of the upper classes . . . Even . . ."

"Exactly! The needle . . ." said Maigret, screwing up his face as the doctor hurt him.

"What do you mean?"

"Planted through the middle of the heart, without a blow being struck, twice in a row—do you think that would imply some knowledge of anatomy?"

The doctor did not answer, and nothing more was said while he replaced the bandages. His face looked careworn. At last he straightened himself with a sigh.

"You say you'd rather be in a hotel?"

"Yes. My wife could come and see to me."

"Are you going to interest yourself in these murders?"

"And how!"

———

Rain would have spoiled everything. But for over a fortnight not a drop fell.

And there was Maigret installed in the best bedroom on the first floor of the Hôtel d' Angleterre. His bed had been shifted over toward one of the windows, and from where he lay he could look down on the place du Marché and watch the sun as it alternately lit up and threw into shadow each row of houses in turn.

Madame Maigret accepted the situation as she accepted everything, without either astonishment or fuss. Within an hour of her arrival the room had become definitely hers. She had brought her own things, added the personal touch.

Two days before, she had been quietly asserting herself in much the same way by her sister's bedside in Alsace.

"A grand girl! If you only could have seen her! Nearly five kilos."

She took the surgeon aside.

"What can he eat, doctor? Some good strong chicken broth? . . . There's one thing you ought to forbid, and that's his pipe. He'll be asking for it before the day's out, as sure as I'm alive. And you should keep him off beer too . . ."

The wallpaper was a marvelous red-and-green affair. Blood red and the crudest of greens, in stripes that fairly hummed in the sunshine.

And horrid little hotel furniture of varnished pitch pine. Nothing that stood squarely on all four legs at once. An immense room with two beds. A mantelpiece two centuries old, in front of which stood a cheap radiator.

"What I'd like to know is what possessed you to do such a thing. Suppose you'd fallen under the train! . . . By the way, I think I'll make you a *crème au citron*. I take it they'll raise no objection to my using the kitchen."

The semiconscious reveries were becoming rarer now. Even with the sun shining through his closed eyelids, Maigret's ideas were fairly logical. Nevertheless he still went on with his puppet show, playing with the characters his imagination had elaborated.

"The first victim . . . the woman from the Moulin-Neuf Farm . . . Married? Any children?

"She had married a farmer's son and lived with the family. She didn't get on any too well with her mother-in-law, who accused her of thinking too much about her looks and wearing silk underclothes—even for milking the cows . . ."

It was something to go on, and Maigret went patiently to work, painting her portrait in his mind as lovingly as any artist could manipulate his brushes. He saw an attractive, buxom, well-washed young woman introducing newfangled ideas into the farmer's household, consulting catalogues that would be sent her from Paris.

She was returning home from the town . . . Maigret could see the road perfectly. It must be, like all the roads round Bergerac, overshadowed by a row of plane trees on either hand . . . And the white, dusty, chalky surface—vibrant even in the weakest sunlight . . .

And then the girl on her bicycle.

"Sixteen. Old enough to have a boyfriend. There was no mention of one, however. Once a year she used to have a fortnight's holiday in Paris, staying with an aunt . . ."

The bed was sweaty. The surgeon came twice a day.

After lunch, Leduc would arrive in his Ford, and make several clumsy attempts to park it under Maigret's window before getting it properly lined up.

On the third morning, he turned up wearing a straw hat, just like the police inspector.

The public prosecutor called, and taking Madame Maigret for a servant, he handed her his hat and stick, and was then profuse in his apologies. In any case, he had come to apologize.

"You see, your not having any papers on you . . . I'm sure you'll forgive the mistake."

"Yes, my pocketbook seems to have disappeared . . . But do sit down . . ."

Even so, the man still looked aggressive. He simply couldn't help it: it had become a habit. Added to the scowl on his face, he had a little bulbous nose and a bristling mustache.

"It's a most lamentable affair. To think that in a place like this! . . . Now, if it had been in Paris, where hooligans and madmen can be met with every day . . . But here! . . ."

Sacrebleu! Here was another man with bushy eyebrows! Like the doctor. Like the peasant. They were gray too. And whether he had seen them or not, Maigret couldn't help attributing thick gray eyebrows to the man in the train.

The head of his stick was of carved ivory.

"Well! Anyhow . . . I hope you'll soon be on your feet again and that you won't bear us a grudge."

He had only come out of politeness and was already longing to go.

"You've an excellent doctor, at all events. A pupil of Martel's . . . As for the rest, it's a pity . . ."

"What rest?"

"Oh! Never mind. No need for you to worry . . . I'll look in again one of these days, and in the meantime they'll let me know how you're getting on."

As soon as he had gone, Maigret started to lap up his *crème au citron,* which was a perfect masterpiece. But the smell of truffles that rose from the kitchen was rather mortifying.

"You never saw such a thing," said his wife. "They serve up truffles by the dishful here, just like fried potatoes. You'd think they were two a penny. Even in the fifteen-franc dinner."

Then it was Leduc's turn.

"Sit down . . . Like some of my *crème au citron*? . . . No? . . . Well, tell me what you know of the private life of my doctor. I haven't even heard his name."

"Dr. Rivaud. I don't know much about him really— that is, apart from gossip. He lives with a wife and a sister-in-law. And they say the sister-in-law is just as much his wife as the real one . . . But of course . . ."

"And the prosecutor?"

"Monsieur Duhourceau. You've heard something already?"

"Go on."

"His sister's the widow of a sea captain, and she's in

an asylum. Though some say she's not mad at all, but that he had her shut up so as to get hold of her money."

Maigret was sitting up in bed, gazing out through the window with half-closed eyes. To Leduc's surprise he beamed with satisfaction.

"And what else?"

"Nothing. In these little towns, you know . . ."

"But don't forget, my dear Leduc, that this little town is different from any other. It's a little town with a madman."

It was quite funny to see Leduc. He seemed really rather upset.

"Yes, a madman. A madman at large. A madman who's only mad by fits and starts, while the rest of the time he's walking about and talking to people, just like anybody else."

"How does Madame Maigret like it here?"

"She's been turning the kitchen upside down. She and the chef exchange recipes. When I come to think of it, perhaps it's the chef who's mad."

There's something slightly intoxicating about a narrow escape from death. And then to lie in bed and be cosseted . . . Especially in an atmosphere of unreality . . .

To lie in bed and let your brain work of itself, just for the fun of it, studying a strange place and strange people through a sunlit window . . .

"I suppose there's a public library in the town?"

"Of course."

"Well, if you want to do me a great favor, you'll go

and pick me out the best books on mental diseases, per-
versions, maniacs, and all the rest of it. And bring me the
telephone directory—they're always most instructive
books. And ask downstairs whether their telephone has
a long cord so that I can have it brought up to my room."

Maigret was drowsy. He could feel the somnolence
welling up from the depths of his being and spreading
gradually to every limb.

"It's Saturday tomorrow. I assume you'll be having
lunch here."

"Of course, and I have to buy a goat!"

Leduc picked up his straw hat. When he shut the
door behind him, Maigret's eyes were closed and his
breathing came regularly through his half-open mouth.

Downstairs, in the passage, the retired inspector ran
into Dr. Rivaud. Drawing the latter aside, he hesitated
and shuffled and then stammered.

"You're quite sure, I suppose, that this wound . . .
that it couldn't have affected my friend's intelligence? . . .
I mean his . . . I hardly know how to put it . . . but perhaps you understand . . ."

The gesture with which the doctor answered might
have meant anything.

"He's an intelligent man as a rule?" he asked.

"Very intelligent, even if he doesn't always look it."

"Ah!"

And with that the surgeon turned thoughtfully and
went upstairs.

THE SECOND-CLASS TICKET

Maigret had left Paris on the previous Tuesday, late in the afternoon. Wounded early on the Wednesday morning, he had spent that day in the hospital of Bergerac. As soon as his wife had arrived, he had been moved to the big first-floor room of the Hôtel d' Angleterre.

On Monday his wife suddenly said to him:

"Why didn't you use your free traveling-pass?"

It was four in the afternoon. Madame Maigret, whose hands were never idle, was tidying up the room for the third time that day.

The place du Marché was humming with life. The outside blinds were partially lowered, giving a mellow light inside the room.

Maigret, who was smoking one of his first pipes, looked at his wife with some astonishment. It seemed to him that she avoided his eye as she waited for his answer. He even thought she was slightly flushed with embarrassment.

It was certainly an unexpected question. Every inspector attached to a flying squad had a railway pass that enabled him to travel free first-class anywhere in France. And of course Maigret had used his last Tuesday.

"Come here and sit down."

He saw she hesitated, but he insisted.

"Now, tell me all about it."

She became still more embarrassed under his quizzical look.

"I oughtn't to have put the question like that . . . But I can't help thinking you're a bit strange at times."

"You too?"

"What do you mean?"

"Well, everybody else does! And they can't bring themselves to believe wholeheartedly in my story of the man in the train . . . And now . . ."

"Listen! It's like this—there's a mat in the passage, outside our door, and when I moved it just now I found this."

Although she was living in a hotel, she wore an apron—she said it made her feel more at home. She now felt in its pocket and drew out a railway ticket. It was a second-class ticket from Paris to Bergerac, and was dated the previous Tuesday.

"Next to the mat . . ." Maigret repeated. "Take a pencil and a piece of paper."

She obeyed, licked the point of the pencil and sat waiting.

"Now, who's been to see me here? . . . First of all, the proprietor of the hotel. He came up around nine in the morning to check on how I was doing. Then the doctor, just before ten . . . Make a list of them . . . The prosecutor came at midday. Then the local inspector arrived when he left . . ."

"There's Leduc," said Madame Maigret reluctantly.

"Quite right! Put him down. Is that all? . . . Of course there are the hotel staff. And, for that matter, anybody staying in the hotel might have dropped it as they went along the passage."

"But there's no reason for them to be in the passage."

"Why not?"

"Because it only leads to this room. If they came as far as our door it would be to look through the keyhole."

"Ring up the stationmaster, will you?"

Maigret had seen practically nothing of the town, and he had not been anywhere near the station. But he had studied the plan in the *Guide Michelin,* and with its help he had formed a mental picture of Bergerac that was accurate in all essentials.

He knew that the place du Marché that he surveyed through his window was at the very heart of the town. The large building on the right was for the most part out of sight, but he knew it nonetheless as the Palais de Justice. Under the heading *Hôtel d' Angleterre,* the guide said:

First class. Rooms from 25 francs. With bathrooms. Meals from 15 to 18 francs. Specialties: truffles, foie gras, boned and rolled chicken, Dordogne salmon.

The Dordogne flowed past behind the hotel, out of sight. Maigret could not only follow its course on the plan, but could study its scenery in a series of picture postcards. Another showed him the outside of the station. As for the Hôtel de France on the other side of the place du Marché, he knew it to be the rival of his own. And he pictured the streets converging on the main roads, just like the one he had recently been staggering along.

"I've got the stationmaster on the phone."

"Ask him if any passengers alighted from the Paris train early Wednesday morning."

"He says no."

"That's all."

It was impossible to come to any other conclusion than that the ticket found in the passage had been used by the man who had jumped from the train.

"Do you know what I'd like you to do? . . . Go and have a look at Monsieur Duhourceau's house—you know, the public prosecutor's. And then you might go and see Dr. Rivaud's.

"What for?"

"Nothing in particular. Just to tell me what you see."

He took advantage of being alone to exceed the number of pipes he was allowed. The day was closing in, the place du Marché rose-colored with evening light. The commercial travelers, having finished their rounds, drove up one after another, parking their cars in front of the hotel. From downstairs came the clack of billiard balls. Others would no doubt be drinking their aperitifs in the bright room downstairs, with the proprietor popping in now and again in his chef's hat to make sure everything was all right.

Why had the fellow risked his neck, or at any rate a broken limb, jumping out of the train? And why had he fired at Maigret?

One thing was certain: the man knew the line. He had opened the door just before the brakes went on. If he couldn't face the station it would be for fear of being recognized. So he was known in Bergerac . . .

Not that that proved him a murderer . . . Maigret recalled his restlessness as he tossed about in the upper couchette, his deep sighs, and the time he tried so desperately to keep still.

"Duhourceau must be home by now. He'll be in his study perhaps, reading the Paris papers. Or he may have brought some work to finish off at home . . . The surgeon will be doing his evening rounds, followed by a sister . . . The police inspector . . ."

He was in no hurry. As a rule, at the beginning of a case, he was all on edge with impatience, but as soon as he had something to go on, as soon as he had decided on his line of action, he was as cool and calm as could be.

But this time it was the opposite, perhaps because of his current state.

He'd have to stay in bed for a fortnight anyhow—wasn't that what the doctor had said? So there was no use being in a hurry. He had plenty of time. Long days with nothing else to do but to make mental pictures of Bergerac and its surroundings and get all the characters into their proper places.

"I should ring for someone to come and turn the light on."

But he was too lazy and didn't bother. By the time Madame Maigret returned, it was quite dark. The window was wide open and a cold breeze blew in. The street lamps made a garland of light round the market-place below.

"Do you want to catch pneumonia?" said Madame Maigret, making straight for the window. "If so, you're going the right way about it. Why didn't you ring and ask them to shut it?"

"Well?"

"Well what? I've seen a couple of houses, but I don't know what good that's going to do us."

"Come on! Tell me what they're like."

"Monsieur Duhourceau lives over on the other side of the Palais de Justice, in a square as big as the place du Marché. A massive three-story house. The first floor has a stone balcony. The room behind it was lit up: I suppose it would be his study. Downstairs there was a manservant closing the shutters."

"Does it look a bright place?"

"Bright? What do you mean? . . . A big house like any other. A somber place, if anything, though the crimson velvet curtains must have cost two thousand francs a window. Soft, silky stuff, but very heavy, falling in big folds . . ."

Maigret chuckled. It was exactly what he wanted. With a few touches he corrected the picture he had already formed in his mind.

"And the servant?"

"The manservant? Yes?"

"Was he wearing a striped waistcoat?"

"He was."

Maigret could have clapped. He could see the place perfectly. A solid, dignified house, richly curtained, a carved stone balcony. Indoors, old furniture and a manservant with a striped waistcoat. The prosecutor himself in a morning coat and gray trousers, patent-leather boots, close-cropped white hair . . .

"That's right, isn't it? He does wear patent-leather boots?"

"Yes. Button boots. I noticed them when he called."

Patent-leather boots! Like the man in the train! But weren't his lace-up boots?

"And now the doctor's house."

"It's almost on the edge of the town. A villa like those you see by the seaside."

"English cottage style?"

"That kind of thing. A low roof, lawns, flower beds, gravel paths. A pretty garage. The shutters are painted green, and there's a wrought-iron lantern hanging over the front door . . . The shutters were still open, and I could see his wife in the drawing room with some needlework."

"And her sister?"

"She drove up with the doctor as I was coming away. She's very young, very pretty, very well dressed. Nothing provincial about her. I'd bet anything her clothes come from Paris . . ."

Interesting. But what had all this to do with a madman who attacked women at night in lonely places, first strangling them, then sticking a needle through their hearts?

Maigret made no attempt to answer that question. He was simply fixing all the characters in place.

"Did you meet anybody?"

"Nobody I knew. The people here don't seem to go out much in the evenings."

"Is there a cinema?"

"I caught sight of one in a side street. They were showing a film I saw in Paris three years ago."

———

Ten o'clock in the morning. Leduc drove up and parked his car below. A moment or two later he knocked at Maigret's door. The latter was smacking his lips over a bowl of beef tea that his wife had made herself.

"How are you getting on?"

"Sit down. No. Not on that chair—you'd block the view."

Since leaving the Police Judiciaire, Leduc had grown

stouter. He had also changed in manner, being gentler and more timid than he used to be.

"What's your cook giving you for lunch today?"

"Lamb cutlets in cream sauce. I have to avoid heavy food."

"Tell me—have you been to Paris recently?"

Madame Maigret looked up sharply, surprised at the bluntness of the question. As for Leduc, his face clouded and he looked at his friend reproachfully.

"What do you mean? . . . You know very well that . . ."

"Of course!"

Maigret knew very well that . . . But he studied Leduc's profile with its little reddish mustache. Then he looked down at his feet, shod in heavy shooting boots.

"Between ourselves, what facilities are there in this part of the world for enjoying the charms of the fair sex?"

"Really!" protested Madame Maigret. "You're letting your tongue run away with you."

"Not at all. It's a most important question. In the country they don't have all the amenities of the town . . . How old is your cook?"

"Sixty-five! So you see . . ."

"No young blood about the place?"

What made it so awkward was the seriousness with which Maigret put the questions, for they were the kind of questions that are usually proffered in a playful, bantering tone.

"No little shepherdess, for instance?"

"There's only the cook's niece who comes from time to time to lend her a hand."

"Sixteen? . . . Eighteen?"

"Nineteen. But really . . . !"

"I see!"

Leduc fidgeted, while Madame Maigret, even more embarrassed than he, withdrew to the darkest corner of the room.

"You're being abominably tactless," she said.

"So that's that!" said Maigret doggedly. For a moment the cross-examination appeared to be over, but after a short silence he grunted:

"Duhourceau's a bachelor, I understand. How does he manage?"

"There's no mistaking you come from Paris. You speak of these things as if they were the most ordinary matters. Do you think the prosecutor relates his peccadiloes to everyone he meets?"

"No. But as everything gets round sooner or later, you're bound to have heard."

"I only know what people say."

"There you are!"

"They say he goes once or twice a week to Bordeaux, where he . . ."

Maigret had not once taken his eyes off his friend's face, and a queer smile floated on his lips. He had known another Leduc, and a much more outspoken one. None of these hesitations and country-town embarrassments.

"Do you know what you ought to do? After all, as you've been in the police yourself, they'd give you plenty of rope . . . Start a little investigation, and see if you can find out who was away from Bergerac last Tuesday. But wait a moment—the people I'm most interested in are Dr. Rivaud, the prosecutor, the police inspector, you, and . . ."

Leduc jumped up from his seat. He looked at his straw hat like a man who is thinking of cramming it on his head and walking out of the room.

"A joke's all very well," he said, "but this one's gone far enough. I really don't know what's come over you. Since you've been wounded you . . . you haven't been yourself at all . . . Are you seriously suggesting that, in a little place like this where the least thing will set tongues wagging . . . that I should take it upon myself to start nosing into the doings of the public prosecutor? And the police inspector? I haven't the smallest right to do so . . . As for your insinuations about myself . . ."

"Sit down, Leduc."

"I haven't much time."

"Sit down, I tell you. Just listen to me and you'll understand. Here in Bergerac is a man who in ordinary life seems perfectly normal and probably exercises some profession, a man who now and again in a fit of madness . . ."

"And you don't hesitate to put me down on the list of possibles! Don't think I didn't see the point of your questions just now. You wanted to know if I had a mistress. Why? Because a man who's unsatisfied is more likely than another to . . ."

He was really angry. He had turned quite red and his eyes were glowing.

"The local police have taken the case in hand. It's nothing whatever to do with me. And if you want to get mixed up in . . ."

". . . in something that is no business of mine! . . . Perhaps you're right, but just imagine that, in two or three days, or four, or five, that little nineteen-year-old of yours is found dead with a needle through her heart."

But Leduc had had enough. This time he really did cram the straw hat onto his head. And he strutted out of the room, shutting the door rather forcefully behind him.

Madame Maigret, waiting for this moment, came up to the bedside. She looked worried, even anxious.

"What on earth has he done to you that you should treat him like that? I've rarely seen you so disagreeable. One might almost think you really suspected him."

"Don't you worry. He'll soon be back—you'll see— and he'll be tumbling over himself trying to make it up. Then I'll ask you to go and have lunch with him at La Ribaudière."

"Me?

But . . ."

"Now, be an angel and fill me a pipe. And these pillows are slipping down again . . ."

Half an hour later, when the doctor came to see him, Maigret smiled benignly. He greeted Rivaud cordially.

"What did he say to you?"

"Who?"

"My friend Leduc. He's rather bothered about me, and I wouldn't mind betting he asked you to check my state of mind. No, doctor, I'm not at all mad, but . . ."

He got no farther, however, as a thermometer was thrust into his mouth. While his temperature was being taken, Dr. Rivaud removed the dressing. The wound was slow in healing.

"You move about too much. There you are! Over a hundred and two. I don't need to ask you if you've been smoking. The air's thick with it."

"You ought to forbid it altogether," said Madame Maigret.

But her husband interrupted her:

"Can you tell me at what intervals our madman's crimes were committed?"

"Let me see . . . The first was a month ago. The second a week later. While the one that miscarried was the following Friday, and . . ."

"Do you know what I think, doctor? . . . That there's a good chance another body will be found in the next day or two. If not, it means the chap feels he's being watched. But if there is another . . ."

"Well?"

"It might enable us to eliminate some people. Suppose, for instance, you were in this room at the moment the crime was committed. That would put you out of the running straight away. Suppose the prosecutor was at Bordeaux, the police inspector in Paris, the landlord downstairs in his kitchen, and Leduc anywhere you like . . ."

The surgeon stared hard at his patient.

"You seem to have restricted the range of possibilities already."

"Probabilities."

"It's all the same. You confine the suspects to the handful of people you've come in contact with."

"Not even as many as that. I've left out the clerk . . . My list is, in fact, restricted to the people who've been to see me here in the hotel and who could inadvertently have dropped a railway ticket. As a matter of fact, where were you last Tuesday?"

"Last Tuesday?"

Taken aback, the doctor groped in his memory. He was still quite a young man, active and ambitious. His movements were decisive. Altogether he cut a very good figure.

"I think . . . wait a moment . . . Yes, I drove over to La Rochelle for . . ."

He broke off, bridling at the sight of the amused expression on Maigret's face.

"Is this an interrogation? In that case I warn you . . ."

"Take it easy, doctor. Don't forget that I've nothing to do the whole day long. And I'm used to living in a whirl of activity. So I've invented a little game to keep my mind busy. It's called 'Madman' . . . And you'll admit that there's nothing to prevent a doctor being a madman, or a madman a doctor. It's even said that all mental specialists are their own patients. Nor is there anything to prevent a public prosecutor . . . ?"

He heard the doctor whisper to Madame Maigret:

"He hasn't been drinking, has he?"

As soon as they were alone together, she came over to her husband's bedside, her brow heavy with reproaches.

"Don't you see what you're doing? . . . I simply can't make you out. You're carrying on exactly as if you wanted everybody to believe you were the madman yourself . . . The doctor didn't say anything—he's too polite—but I could see . . . And now what are you smiling about?"

"Nothing. The sunshine. Those red and green stripes on the wallpaper. The women chattering in the marketplace. That little lemon yellow car that looks like some huge insect . . . and then the smell of foie gras . . . Only, of course—somewhere or other—there's a madman . . . There! Look at that girl. Little pear-shaped breasts and calves as stout as any mountaineer's. Why shouldn't the madman choose her next?"

Madame Maigret looked into his eyes and she could see he was not joking any longer. On the contrary, he was speaking with intense seriousness. There was even a note of real trouble in his voice. He took hold of her hand before going on:

"You see, I don't think it's over. And I don't want . . . I don't want that fine young girl to pass under my window next time in a hearse, followed by a lot of people in black . . . Yes, there's a madman about. A man who laughs and talks, who comes and goes . . ."

Maigret's eyes were half-closed now. In a coaxing voice he murmured:

"Give me a pipe all the same."

4

MAIGRET'S RECEPTION

Maigret had chosen nine o'clock in the morning because it was his favorite time of the day. He loved the quality of morning sunshine, loved the sounds that made the start of a day's activity—doors opening and shutting, the early traffic in the street, the footfalls on the pavements—sounds that would steadily increase in volume to their midday climax.

Through his window he could see on a plane tree one of the notices he had had posted up in various parts of the town:

At 9 a.m. on Wednesday morning, at the Hôtel d' Angleterre, Inspector Maigret will give 100 francs reward to anyone giving information concerning the murders that have recently been committed in the neighborhood of Bergerac, apparently by some demented person.

"Shall I stay?" asked Madame Maigret, who, even in a hotel, found almost as much to keep her busy as she did in her own house.

"Yes, you can stay."

"I'm not particularly anxious to. But in any case I don't expect anyone will come."

Maigret smiled. Half past eight had struck only a moment before, yet, as he lit his pipe, he muttered:

"Here's one already."

It was the familiar sound of the old Ford, which they recognized as soon as it came over the bridge.

"Why didn't Leduc come yesterday?"

"Because of our little exchange. We don't see eye to eye about the Madman of Bergerac, but that won't prevent his being here in a moment."

"Who? The madman?"

"Leduc. But maybe the madman too. Or possibly several madmen. In fact there's every chance. A notice like the one I've had put up exerts a fatal attraction on every unbalanced or overimaginative person . . . Come in, Leduc."

The latter hadn't even had time to knock. There was a somewhat contrite look on his face.

"You couldn't come yesterday?"

"No. Do forgive me . . . Good morning, Madame Maigret . . . A pipe burst and I had to fetch a plumber . . . Feeling better?"

"Fine, thanks, except for my back, which is stiff as a poker. Have you seen my notice?"

"What notice?"

He was lying, and Maigret was on the point of chaffing him about it. In the end, however, he decided to be merciful.

"Give my wife your hat, and come and sit down. I'm holding a reception here shortly, and I've even invited the madman himself."

There was a knock at the door, though no steps had been heard entering the hotel. It was the landlord.

"Excuse me. I didn't know you had a visitor . . . It's about that notice."

"You've something to tell me?"

"Me? Certainly not. If I'd had anything to tell you I wouldn't have waited till you offered a reward. What I wanted to ask was whether we were to show up everybody who comes."

"By all means."

Maigret looked at the man with half-closed eyes. Screwing his eyes up was becoming quite a habit with him. Or was it merely that the sun was in his eyes?

"Yes. Show them all up." And when the landlord had gone he turned to Leduc and went on:

"He's a queer chap too. Strong as a bull and red as raw beef. One of those florid people who look as though they might burst at any moment."

"Started life as a farm laborer somewhere round here. Then he married his employer, a woman of forty-five. He was no more than twenty."

"And since then?"

"This is his third marriage. He is cursed. All his wives have died."

"He'll he back again presently."

"Why?"

"Hanged if I know. But he'll come all right—when everybody's here. He'll find some pretext or other. The prosecutor will be leaving home around now. As for the doctor, you can take it from me he's dashing round the wards as fast as his legs will carry him. He won't linger over his rounds this morning."

Maigret had hardly finished his sentence when Monsieur Duhourceau emerged from a side street and toddled across the place du Marché.

"That makes three."

"How do you reckon three?"

"The prosecutor, the landlord . . . and you."

"Still on that tack? Look here, Maigret! . . ."

"Hush! Open the door to Monsieur Duhourceau. He can't make up his mind to knock."

"I'll be back in an hour or two," said Madame Maigret, who had put on her hat.

The prosecutor bowed ceremoniously to her as she crossed him at the doorway, then came forward to shake Maigret's hand—without, however, looking him in the face.

"I heard about your experiment and I thought I'd better see you first. Of course it's understood that you're acting in a private capacity. Even so, I should like to have been consulted, considering this is a case that is being investigated officially."

"Sit down, won't you? Leduc, take the prosecutor's hat and stick. I was just telling Leduc that the killer is bound to turn up . . . Ah! Here comes the inspector looking at his watch and wondering whether he'll have a drink downstairs before coming up."

It was the truth. They saw him enter the hotel, but it was not till ten minutes later that he knocked at the bedroom door. He was disconcerted to find the prosecutor there, and felt called upon to explain his presence . . .

"I thought it my duty to . . ."

"Naturally," broke in Maigret cheerily. "We'll be wanting another chair, Leduc. Perhaps you'll find one in the room next door . . . I think I can see some of our customers gathering below. Only, no one wants to be the first."

There were indeed three or four people wandering about in the place du Marché, throwing frequent glances in the direction of the hotel. In fact, they looked exactly as if they were summoning up their courage. All of them stared at the doctor's car as it drew up at the entrance.

In spite of the spring sunshine, there was an atmosphere of nervousness. The surgeon, like the others, was disconcerted not to find Maigret alone.

"Quite a council of war!" he said, with none too pleasant a smile.

Maigret noticed that he was badly shaved, and his tie suggested hasty dressing.

"Do you think we might expect the examining magistrate?" asked Maigret.

"He's away for the day," answered the inspector, "conducting an inquiry at Saintes."

"Has he taken his clerk with him?"

"I don't know if he took him along . . . No, wait . . . There he is coming out now. He lives just opposite in that house with the blue shutters."

There were steps in the passage. Two or three people were approaching. Then the steps ceased and there were loud whisperings.

"Open the door, Leduc."

The woman who entered was not one of the people who had been gathering in the place du Marché. She was one of the chambermaids of the hotel, the one who had had such a narrow escape from the madman's hands. Following her was a shy, awkward young man with fair hair.

"This is my fiancé. He works in the garage . . . He didn't like the idea of my coming here. He thinks the less said, the better."

"Come right in, and your fiancé . . . And you too if you like."

The last words were addressed to the landlord, who was standing in the passage, his chef's cap in his hand.

"I just came up to see whether my maid . . ."

"Yes, come in. And what is your name, young lady?"

"Rosalie, monsieur. Only I don't know whether I'd be entitled to the reward, seeing as I've told the police everything already."

The fiancé stared angrily in front of him and muttered:

"Assuming it's true . . ."

"Of course it's true. Do you think I'd have invented it?"

"I suppose it's true that a rich gentleman proposed to you! And that your mother was brought up by the gypsies!"

The girl was furious, but she wasn't going to give in. A buxom peasant girl with firm flesh and brawny limbs. Her hair would go out of place when she moved about, like she had been in a battle. When she lifted her arms to smooth it down, she revealed the red hair in her moist armpits.

"I won't take back a word of it . . . He came up behind me. I suddenly felt a hand slipping round under my chin. So I bit it for all I was worth. Wait a moment— there was a gold ring on one of the fingers . . ."

"You didn't see him?"

"Not properly. He dashed off into the trees, so I only saw his back view. And I'd hardly had time to pick myself up and get my breath back."

"You wouldn't be able to recognize him, then? I think you said so to the police."

Rosalie did not answer. There was an obstinate, hostile look on her face.

"Would you recognize the ring?"

And Maigret's eye wandered round the room, resting for a moment on one after the other of his guests' hands: Leduc's pudgy ones with their heavy signet ring; the long graceful hands of Dr. Rivaud with only a wedding ring; Duhourceau's with white parched skin, which were fidgeting with a handkerchief he had just taken from his pocket.

"A gold ring," she repeated sullenly.

"And you've no idea who it was that assaulted you?"

"Can I say something, monsieur?" pleaded the fiancé, his forehead beaded with sweat.

"Fire away."

"I don't want Rosalie to get into trouble. She's a good girl, and I say it to her face. But she has dreams every night. Sometimes she tells me them. And sometimes she'll tell me the same thing again a few days later just as if it had really happened. It's the same when she reads a story."

"Fill me a pipe, Leduc, will you?"

Through the window, Maigret could see a group of at least ten people talking in undertones in front of the hotel.

"So you really have no idea, Rosalie?"

The girl said nothing. But her eyes rested for a second on the public prosecutor, whose patent-leather boots caught Maigret's eye once more.

"Give her a hundred francs, Leduc. You don't mind acting as my secretary, do you? . . . Are you satisfied with her?" he asked the landlord.

"She's a good maid. I can't say she isn't."

"Right! Send in the next."

The examining magistrate's clerk had meanwhile

worked his way into the room and was standing against the wall.

"Oh! So you've come? Find yourself a chair if you can."

"I'm afraid I haven't much time," said the doctor, looking at his watch.

"Go on! Time enough!"

And Maigret lit his pipe with his eyes on the door, which opened to admit a young man. He had oozing eyes and a mop of stringy hair, and was dressed in rags.

"I trust you're not going to . . ." muttered the prosecutor.

"Come in, my boy. When did you have your last fit?"

"He left the hospital a week ago," said the doctor.

An obvious epileptic, the type of creature who, in the country, is inevitably regarded as the village idiot.

"What have you got to tell me?"

"Me?"

"Yes, you. Spit it out."

But instead of speaking, the wretch burst into tears. After a moment his sobs became so convulsive that he seemed on the verge of another attack. At last, between them, he managed to stammer:

"They're always down on me . . . I've done nothing . . . I swear I haven't . . . So why shouldn't I have a hundred francs like the others . . . to buy myself a suit with."

"A hundred francs," said Maigret to Leduc. "Next, please."

The prosecutor was visibly losing patience, while the police inspector pretended to be bored.

"If *we* dealt out money like that," he murmured, "we'd have the council down on us in no time."

Rosalie and her young man, who were still in the room, were fighting it out in angry whispers in a corner. The landlord put his head out the door to listen for any others who might be coming in downstairs.

"Are you really expecting to find something out?" sighed Monsieur Duhourceau.

"Oh, dear, no . . . Nothing at all."

"In that case . . ."

"I told you the madman would be here, and it is quite likely that he is."

Only three more people came in: first, a road worker, who three days previously had seen a "shadow flitting between the trees."

"Did the shadow do anything to you?"

"No."

"And you couldn't recognize him, of course . . . Fifty francs for the shadow, Leduc. That's quite enough."

Maigret was the only one to keep his good humor. There were now two or three dozen people below, gathered in little groups, throwing curious glances up at the windows of the hotel.

"And you?"

It was an old peasant, dressed in mourning, who had been waiting with a dull scowl on his face.

"I'm the father of the first one. Yes, it was my lass

that was the first to be killed. And I've come to tell you that if ever I set hands on that monster, I'll . . ."

His eyes too rested for a moment on the public prosecutor.

"You've no idea, I suppose?"

"Well, I wouldn't call it an idea. But I'm not afraid to speak my mind. They wouldn't dare touch a man as had lost his daughter . . . And what I say is, why don't they look in the right place? Why don't they look where there's been trouble before? . . . You're a stranger to the place. You don't know . . . But anybody could tell you there's been things going on that no one's ever found the answer to . . ."

Dr. Rivaud had risen to his feet and was shifting restlessly about. The police inspector looked aside and pretended not to be listening. As for the prosecutor, he seemed turned to stone.

"Many thanks, old man."

"And I'll tell you this, that I don't want any of your hundred francs or your fifty francs either . . . But if you should ever pass my way . . . Anybody'll tell you where my place is . . ."

He didn't ask if he might go. Without so much as a nod of farewell he slouched away, and his rounded shoulders disappeared through the doorway.

His departure was followed by a long silence, during which Maigret was apparently preoccupied with his pipe, pressing down the half-burnt tobacco with his one serviceable hand.

"Strike me a match, Leduc."

A silence that had something touching in it, and which appeared to have also taken hold of the people standing in the place du Marché, who seemed fixed in an unnatural stillness.

No sound but the steps of the old peasant crunching the gravel below, and then:

"For God's sake hold your tongue . . ."

It was Rosalie's fiancé who spoke, not realizing he had said the words out loud. Rosalie stared straight in front of her with pursed lips, perhaps obediently, or perhaps only biding her time.

"Well, gentlemen," sighed Maigret at last, "that's not so bad for a start, is it?"

"We've been through all this already," said the police inspector, picking up his hat and rising.

Maigret ignored the reproof. He looked at nobody. Gazing at his counterpane, he said:

"Do you think, doctor, that after an attack has passed, the madman would remember what he's done?"

"It's practically certain."

The landlord was standing in the middle of the room now, feeling very conspicuous in his white clothes.

"Have a look outside the door, Leduc. See if there's anybody else."

"You must excuse me," said Dr. Rivaud, "but I really must be going. I've an appointment at eleven, and it too is a question of life and death."

"I'll come down with you," said the police inspector.

"And what about you, *monsieur le procureur*?"

"Hum! . . . Yes . . . I think I . . ."

Somehow Maigret seemed dissatisfied. He kept glancing out of the window. Everyone was standing, and on the point of going.

But Maigret, raising himself slightly in the bed, said quietly:

"One moment, gentlemen . . . I don't think we're finished yet."

He pointed to a woman who was crossing the place du Marché at a run. The surgeon could see her from where he stood and exclaimed:

"Françoise!"

"You know her?"

"She's my sister-in-law . . . She must be coming to fetch me. An urgent call. Some accident, I suppose."

There were voices below and hurried steps on the stairs. Then the door opened and Françoise burst breathless into the room, staring wild-eyed around her.

"Jacques! . . . Inspector! . . . *Monsieur le procureur!* . . ."

She was young, hardly past twenty, slim, pretty, and nervous.

But her dress was covered in dust, and even torn in one place. Instinctively she kept putting her hands to her neck.

"I . . . I've seen him . . . He tried to . . ."

She could hardly get the words out. Everyone stood still, staring at her. Then she went up to her brother-in-law.

"Look!"

She showed him her neck. There were marks on it.

"It was over in the Moulin-Neuf Wood . . . I was walking along when a man . . ."

"I thought we'd find out something," said Maigret, who had quite recovered his equanimity. Leduc, who really knew him very well, looked at him, puzzled.

"You saw him, I suppose?"

"Not very well. I don't know how I managed to shake him off. I think he must have tripped over a root. Anyhow, he loosened his grip for a second and I broke free . . . I hit him . . ."

"Describe him."

"I hardly know how to. Some sort of a tramp. Dressed like any peasant. His ears stuck out . . . One thing I'm sure of—it was no one I'd ever seen before."

"He ran away?"

"I heard a car passing along the road. He must have heard it too . . . And he knew I was going to shout . . . In a second he disappeared into a thicket."

She was getting her breath back, though she still panted, with one hand on her breast, the other at her neck.

"My God, I had a fright . . . If it hadn't been for that car . . . I didn't stop running all the way here."

"But wouldn't it have been shorter to go home?"

"I knew there was nobody there except my sister."

"Were you to the left of the farm?" asked the local inspector.

"A little beyond the old quarry."

"I'll have the wood searched at once. It's not too late," the inspector said to the prosecutor.

Dr. Rivaud looked annoyed. With a frown on his face he studied the girl, who was now leaning on the table, breathing more normally. There was a spark of mockery in Leduc's eye as he caught Maigret's. And he couldn't help saying:

"This proves one thing anyhow, and that is that the madman didn't accept your invitation after all."

The inspector went downstairs and hurried across to the police station in the town hall. The prosecutor stood slowly brushing his bowler with his sleeve. Then he turned to Françoise.

"As soon as the examining magistrate returns, I must ask you to go and see him. He'll take a statement from you, which you'll have to sign."

He held his dry hand out to Maigret.

"I suppose you don't want us anymore?"

"It was good of you to come. I had no right to expect it."

At a sign from Maigret, Leduc cleared the room. Rosalie and her young man were still sparring as they left. Returning to the bedside with a smile on his lips, he was surprised to see an anxious expression on his friend's face.

"Well?"

"Nothing."

"It didn't work, did it?"

"On the contrary. It worked too well! Fill me another pipe, will you, before my wife comes back?"

"But I thought you were expecting the madman here?"

"I was."

"But . . ."

"Let's not talk about it now . . . You know, it would be dreadful if there was to be another murder. Because this time . . ."

"What?"

"Never mind. Don't try to understand. Here's my wife crossing the marketplace. She'll say I've been smoking too much and take away the tobacco. Take a bit out of the pouch and stuff it under the pillow."

He was hot. No doubt his temperature was up again.

"Leave me now, if you don't mind . . . Just put the telephone there where I can reach it."

"I'm having lunch here today. It's always good on Thursdays. Goose in aspic . . . I'll look in again before I go."

"Do . . . By the way, about that girl—you know, the one you spoke to me about—is it long since you saw her?"

Leduc bristled. Staring hard into Maigret's eyes, he snapped:

"We've had enough of that."

And he went downstairs, leaving his straw hat on the table.

5

PATENT-LEATHER BOOTS

"Yes, madame . . . The Hôtel d' Angleterrre . . . But please understand that you are perfectly free not to come . . ."

Leduc had left. Madame Maigret was climbing the stairs. Dr. Rivaud was standing by his car in front of the hotel, with his sister-in-law and the prosecutor.

It was to Madame Rivaud that Maigret was telephoning. Françoise had said she was alone in the house. He asked her to come and see him. It did not surprise him in the least to find that the voice at the other end of the line was an anxious one.

Madame Maigret listened to the end of the conversation as she took off her hat.

"Is it true what they say—that there's been another assault? I met some people who were hurrying off to the wood."

Maigret was too absorbed in his own thoughts to answer. The aspect of the town seemed to change under his eyes as the news spread rapidly. More and more people were hurrying down a street that branched off on the left of the place du Marché.

"Isn't there a level crossing along there?" asked Maigret, who was beginning to know the topography of the town.

"Yes, it's a long street that changes gradually into a country road. Moulin-Neuf is after the second turning. In spite of its name, there's no mill there now, only a large whitewashed farm. When I passed, they were harnessing some oxen to a cart. The farmyard was full of poultry, including some fine young turkeys."

Maigret listened like a blind man to whom a landscape is being described.

"Is it a big farm?"

"They measure land in *journaux* in these parts. Two hundred *journaux*, they told me—but it means nothing to me. The wood begins just beyond the house. Farther on you come to the main road to Périgueux."

Doubtless the country gendarmes were out there by now. Maigret could imagine them slowly combing the wood like game beaters. And groups of people held back on the road, children climbing up trees.

"I think you'd better go back. I'd like you to be on the spot."

Without a murmur she put her hat on again. Downstairs in the hall, she crossed a young woman who was coming in. She turned to look at her critically, perhaps not altogether benevolently.

It was Madame Rivaud.

"Do sit down . . . I hope you'll forgive my having bothered you, particularly for so little. For I'm not even sure I've any questions to ask you. It's such a complicated business . . ."

He kept his eyes riveted on her, and she sat before him as though hypnotized. Maigret was puzzled by her, but not altogether astonished. He had somehow guessed that he would find her interesting, but she was a more curious specimen than he had dared to expect.

Her sister Françoise was slim and elegant. Certainly there was nothing provincial about her.

Madame Rivaud was not nearly so good-looking. In fact, she could not have been called attractive at all. She was between twenty-five and thirty, neither tall nor short, but definitely on the stout side. Her clothes must have been made by a pretty humble dressmaker; if not, she didn't know how to wear them.

But what excited Maigret's interest were her eyes. Sad eyes. Anxious eyes. Yet for all their anxiety, there was resignation in them, too.

She looked at Maigret. She was obviously frightened, yet fear seemed only to paralyze her. With a little exaggeration one could say that she sat as though expecting to be hit.

It was impossible to imagine her as anything but a model of country-town respectability. She was fidgeting with her handkerchief. No doubt she would be dabbing her eyes with it on the first suitable occasion.

"How long have you been married, madame?"

She didn't answer at once. The question frightened her. Everything frightened her.

"Five years," she said at last in a dull voice.

"Were you already living in Bergerac?"

Again she looked at Maigret for a considerable time before answering:

"I was living in Algiers with my mother and sister."

Maigret found it quite difficult to go on. The least word seemed to scare her.

"And Dr. Rivaud was living there too?"

"He spent two years at the hospital there."

Maigret was studying her hands. Somehow they didn't seem the right hands for a doctor's wife. Surely those hands had known rough work. How could he maneuver the conversation tactfully on to that subject?

"Your mother . . ." he began.

But he didn't finish the sentence. Madame Rivaud was sitting with her face to the window. And all at once she jumped from her chair, looking more frightened than ever. The door of a car slammed below.

It was Dr. Rivaud, who dashed into the hotel and up the stairs, gave one knock on the door, and burst straight in.

"What are you doing here?"

He spoke to his wife in a hard, dry voice without a glance at Maigret. It was only after a moment that he turned to him to say:

"What's the meaning of this? If you wanted to see my wife, why couldn't you speak to me about it?"

She hung her head, while Maigret assumed an expression of innocent astonishment.

"Really, doctor! . . . What is there to be so angry about? I felt I'd like to make Madame Rivaud's acquaintance. As I'm tied to my bed, I asked her here."

"Have you finished interrogating her?"

"There's been no interrogation, doctor. Merely a little friendly chat. When you arrived we had just got on to the subject of Algiers. Did you like it out there?"

Maigret spoke in a leisurely, offhand way, but his casualness was only on the surface. In reality he was mustering all the energy he possessed, determined to let nothing escape him as he studied the two people before him. Madame Rivaud seemed on the verge of tears, while her husband's eye roved over the room as though looking for some clue to the conversation that had been taking place.

Of one thing Maigret was sure. There was a secret.

What could it be? The public prosecutor was hiding something too. Whatever it was, it was something very complicated and obscure.

"Tell me, doctor—was Madame Rivaud your patient? Is that how you came to know her?"

The surgeon shot a swift glance at his wife.

"I may as well tell you at once that that is of no importance whatever. And now, if you don't mind, I'll drive my wife home, and . . ."

"Obviously . . ."

"Obviously what?"

"Nothing . . . I beg your pardon . . . I hardly realized I was speaking out loud." And then Maigret went on: "This is a strange business, doctor. Very strange. And alarming. The deeper I get into it the more alarming I find it . . . Your sister-in-law must have had a nasty scare. It was marvelous how she managed to pull herself together so quickly. She's plucky."

Rivaud stood there uneasily, waiting for Maigret to go on, the latter watching him narrowly. Wasn't he thinking that the detective knew a good deal more than he pretended?

At last Maigret actually felt he was making headway. But in a moment all the theories he had so laboriously constructed were dashed to the ground.

It began with a gendarme cycling across the place du Marché toward the public prosecutor's office, which he entered. An instant later the telephone rang. Maigret took it.

"Hallo! . . . This is the hospital . . . Is Dr. Rivaud there? . . ."

The doctor took the receiver nervously from Maigret's hand. He listened, thunderstruck, then slowly replaced it, staring vacantly before him.

"They've found him," he said at last.

"Who?"

"The man . . . Or rather his corpse . . . In the Moulin-Neuf Wood."

Madame Rivaud's glance flitted from one to the other of the two men.

"They're asking me to do the postmortem. But . . ."

An idea seemed to strike him. It was now his turn to look suspiciously at Maigret.

"When you were shot the other night in the wood . . . you fired back . . . naturally?"

"I didn't have time to."

But now another idea struck the doctor. He passed his hand in bewilderment across his forehead.

"They think the man's been dead several days. In that case . . . this morning . . . how could Françoise . . . ?"

Then, turning to his wife, he said:

"Come on."

She followed him dutifully, and a minute later their car drove off. Monsieur Duhourceau must have telephoned for a taxi, for an empty one drew up and waited at his door. The gendarme who had brought him the news reappeared and cycled off. After this morning's air of curiosity, the town was now gripped by a more feverish mood.

It was quite a stream of people that poured into the street leading to Moulin-Neuf, including the landlord of the Hôtel d' Angleterre.

But there was Maigret glued to his bed, with a back

that was stiff from being always in the same position, staring ponderously out on to the sun-bathed market-place.

———

"What's the matter?"

"Nothing."

As Madame Maigret came in, she could only see her husband's profile, but that was enough. She knew very well he was out of humor. Nor was she long to guess the cause of it. She came to the bed, and without another word picked up his pipe and began filling it.

"That's better, isn't it?" she said when it was lit. "Now, listen to me and I'll try and tell you all about it. I was there when they found the body, and the gendarmes let me come quite close."

Maigret still stared out of the window. It wasn't the place du Marché, however, that he really saw, but other images that were imprinted on his retina.

"The wood is on a slope at that point. There are oaks alongside the road, then pine trees behind. People were arriving all the time, some by car, some on foot. They'd called out the gendarmes from all the villages around, so as to have the wood completely surrounded . . . The police from here advanced slowly, accompanied by the old farmer from the Moulin-Neuf, who was holding a service revolver. The gendarmes didn't dare say a word . . . I believe he would have shot the killer . . ."

In his mind Maigret conjured up the wood—the

earth covered with pine needles and mottled with patches of light and shade, the gendarmes' uniforms showing between the trees.

"Then we heard a shout, and there was a boy standing, pointing to something at the foot of a tree."

"Patent-leather boots?"

"Yes. And thick gray socks, hand-knitted. I looked specially, as I thought of what you'd told me."

"How old?"

"About fifty. It's hard to say. He was lying face downward . . . and when they raised the head I simply couldn't help looking away. You understand. He'd been lying there for a good week—at least that's what they were saying . . . I waited until they covered his head with a cloth. It seems that no one recognizes him, so he appears to be a stranger."

"Was he wounded?"

"A huge hole in the side of his head."

"What are they doing now?"

"They're chiefly busy keeping back the crowd, which is getting thicker every moment. They've sent for the prosecutor and Dr. Rivaud. After they've seen the body on the spot, they'll move it to the hospital for the postmortem."

The place du Marché was emptier than Maigret had ever seen it. The only creature who seemed quite happy to be there was a little coffee-colored dog that basked in the sun, unconcerned.

Twelve struck with slow strokes. A crowd of working men and women streamed out of a printing works in one of the side streets, most of them on bicycles. With one accord they turned toward Moulin-Neuf.

"How was he dressed?"

"In black. At least the overcoat was. But I really can't say very much. It wasn't a pleasant sight to stare at."

She felt sick at the thought of it. But that didn't prevent her saying:

"Would you like me to go back?"

———

Once more Maigret was alone. He saw the landlord crossing the marketplace. From the pavement the latter called out to him:

"You've heard the news, I suppose? . . . And to think I've got to come back and see to the lunch!"

Then silence, the clear sky above, the empty houses and the sunny marketplace.

It was not till an hour had passed that the sound of an approaching crowd was audible. The body was being taken to the hospital, escorted by half the population of Bergerac. The place du Marché was soon swarming. The hotel filled up, and the clink of glasses rose from the ground floor.

A timid knock on Maigret's door. Leduc put his head in, hesitated, smiled a little awkwardly.

"May I come in?"

He sat down by the bed and lit his meerschaum pipe in silence. Then at last he sighed:

"Well, well! . . . So there we are!"

He was disconcerted, when Maigret turned toward him, to see the broad grin on his face. Still more when the latter said:

"Pleased?"

"But . . ."

"Come, come? You all are. You, the doctor, the prosecutor, the police inspector—all of you delighted at the way I've been made a fool of. That troublesome detective from Paris! Thought he'd chuck his weight about, did he? Thought himself very clever! Worse still, other people began to think he might be. And some people began to be quite nervous about it . . ."

"You admit . . . ?"

"That I was mistaken?"

"Well, they've found the man, haven't they? And he corresponds to your description of the man in the train. I saw the body myself. A middle-aged man. Rather badly dressed, though respectably. There's a bullet hole in the side of the head, and it seems to have been fired at close quarters."

"Yes . . ."

"So close that Monsieur Duhourceau and the police agree that everything points to suicide. They think it was quite a week ago, perhaps immediately after he shot you."

"They found a gun beside him, then?"

"No. That's the only snag. There was a revolver in his pocket, and with only one cartridge fired."

"The one that so nearly did for me."

"That's what they want to find out . . . Certainly, if it's suicide, it goes a long way to clearing up the case. Realizing someone was after him, he felt the game was up, and . . ."

"And if it's not suicide?"

"There are other possible explanations. He may have assaulted someone who was armed, someone who killed him quite properly in self-defense, but was nevertheless too frightened to say anything about it . . . It would be just like these country people."

"And Françoise. What about her little adventure of this morning?"

"We hadn't forgotten that. We think it might have been no more than a spiteful practical joke."

"I see," said Maigret, blowing a ring of smoke toward the ceiling. "What everyone wants is to get the case over and done with as speedily as possible."

"It's not that . . . But you must see that there's really no point in dragging things on . . . now that . . ."

Maigret laughed out loud at his friend's embarrassment.

"There's still that second-class ticket I told you about. Somebody'll have to find an explanation for that. How did it jump out of a dead man's pocket into a passage of the Hôtel d' Angleterre?"

Leduc stared stonily at the crimson carpet. After a long pause he said:

"Do you want some good advice?"

"To let the whole thing drop! That's it, isn't it? To set

my mind on getting well and clear out of Bergerac as soon as I'm fit to travel . . ."

"And come and spend a few days with me at La Ribaudière, as you were intending to do in the first place. I've spoken to Dr. Rivaud about it, and he says that, with proper precautions, there's no reason why you shouldn't be moved now."

"What does the prosecutor say?"

"I don't understand . . ."

"Oh, I'm sure he had something to say about it. Didn't he say that this case had nothing to do with me, except insofar as I was a victim?"

Poor Leduc! He was trying so hard to put it nicely. He wanted to smooth down everybody. But Maigret was being as pigheaded as could be.

"You must realize that according to the regulations . . ." Then, suddenly plucking up his courage, he burst out:

"Listen to me, old chap. I may as well put it plainly. With that little comedy of yours this morning, you've succeeded in putting everybody's back up. The prosecutor has dinner with the prefect every Thursday, and he says he'll speak about you, so that you have your knuckles rapped by your superiors in Paris. What irritated them more than anything was the way you chucked those hundred-franc notes about. They say . . ."

"That I'm encouraging the dregs of the population to wag their tongues."

"How do you know?"

"That I'm inciting them to sling mud at respectable people."

Leduc relapsed into silence. Yes, that was exactly what they said, and what's more, he couldn't help agreeing with them. It was some time before he began again timidly:

"If only you had some real idea to work on, I'd feel differently about it, but . . ."

"But I haven't . . . Or rather I've four or five. Two of them looked very promising this morning. Then all of a sudden they went up in smoke."

"You see! . . . And there's another thing. What possessed you to telephone to Madame Rivaud? You couldn't have made a greater blunder. You've made Rivaud an enemy for life . . . He's so jealous of her that few people can boast of having exchanged a word with her. He hardly lets her out of the house."

"Yet Françoise is his mistress. Why should he be jealous of one but not of the other?"

"I don't know. I can't explain it. It's true she goes about freely enough. Even drives about all alone in the car. Perhaps he makes a distinction between mistresses and wives. You never know . . . Anyhow, I heard him say to the prosecutor that your asking her here was gross bad manners, and that he was itching to teach you a lesson."

"That's a happy thought!"

"What do you mean?"

"He has every opportunity. He dresses my wound twice a day."

Maigret laughed a little too heartily for it to seem altogether on the right side of his face. He laughed like a man who knows he's got himself in a mess, but who knows also that it's too late to withdraw, and that the only thing left him is to put as good a face on it as possible.

"Aren't you going to have lunch? I thought you said something about goose in aspic."

He laughed again. There was a thrilling hand waiting to be played. There were places to go: the woods, the hospital, the Moulin-Neuf Farm, the doctor's house, and the public prosecutor's, so stern and shuttered-up, no doubt. Everywhere, in short. And there was goose in aspic and truffles to eat, and a whole town Maigret hadn't ever seen!

But Maigret was forced to lie there, tied to his bed, with the same little scene in front of him the whole livelong day . . . And every time he made an incautious movement, he almost yelled with the pain. And he even had to have his pipes filled for him, and his wife took advantage of it to cut his smoking down . . .

"Well? What do you think about it? Will you come to my place?"

"I'd love to . . . But not till it's all over."

"But now that our madman's dead . . ."

"Who knows? Run along and have your lunch, and if they ask you what I intend to do, say you don't know . . . And now to work!"

He said it exactly as if he had some heavy manual job to perform, like kneading dough or heavy digging.

As a matter of fact, he had a lot of digging to do, but it was a rather different sort of excavation. It wasn't spadefuls of earth that he had to turn over, but mental images, faces. Faces more than anything.

There was the prosecutor's face with its mixture of fierceness and cold disdain. The doctor's worried face. And the rather insipid features of his wife's. What would he have been treating her for in the hospital at Algiers? . . . Françoise, slight, pretty, and eager . . . And Rosalie dreaming all night—to her young man's despair. Were they already sleeping together? . . . That look of hers at Monsieur Duhourceau—was there something that had been hushed up? . . . And the man who had jumped from the moving train, only to shoot Maigret and die himself . . . Leduc and his housekeeper's niece—it can easily land you in a mess, that sort of thing . . . The landlord of the Hôtel d' Angleterre had already buried two wives and looked hefty enough to kill twenty . . .

Why did Françoise—or rather why was Dr. Rivaud jealous of his wife but not of her? Why was Leduc always beating about the bush? . . . Why? . . . Why? . . . Why? . . .

And now they wanted to ship Maigret off to La Ribaudière as quickly as possible.

He laughed once again, a fat contented laugh, and when Madame Maigret came into the room a quarter of an hour later, she found him blissfully asleep.

THE SEAL

Maigret was in the throes of a harassing dream. The heat was terrible and the low tide had laid bare an immense stretch of sand the color of ripe red corn. There was more sand than sea; in fact, there was hardly any sea at all. It must be out there somewhere, far away in the distance, but all that could be seen were little pools scattered here and there in the otherwise unbroken stretch of sand.

Was Maigret a seal? Perhaps not quite—but neither was he a whale. Probably something between the two. Some large animal, anyhow—a large round shiny lump lying on the sand.

He was all alone in that endless hot expanse. And it was absolutely necessary that he should by some means or other reach the sea, where at last he would be free.

Only he couldn't move. He had flippers like a seal, but he didn't know how to use them. Besides, his whole body was stiff and heavy. If he did manage to raise himself a little, it was only to sink down again on to the burning sand.

Worse still, the sand was soft, and with every movement he sank in a little deeper.

At all costs he must reach the sea. Why was it he was so stiff and heavy? He had a vague idea some man had shot him. But he couldn't remember clearly. He was a big, black, sweating, helpless lump.

———————

When he opened his eyes he saw a bright rectangle of sunshine. It made him blink. Then he saw his wife having breakfast, at the same time keeping a watchful eye on him.

And from the look in her eye, he knew at once that something was amiss. He knew that look well: a grave, maternal, slightly worried look.

"Are you feeling bad?" she asked.

The next thing that struck him was that his head was very heavy.

"Why do you ask?"

"Why indeed? You've been heaving and groaning all night long."

She came over to the bed to kiss him good morning.

"You're looking rotten," she went on. "I suppose you've been having nightmares."

The word at once reminded him of the seal. What a funny dream! He was split between a vague disquiet and a desire to laugh. But he didn't laugh. Sitting on the edge of his bed, Madame Maigret began talking gently, as though afraid of rubbing him up the wrong way.

"We really must come to a decision . . ."

"What decision?"

"Leduc and I were talking things over yesterday. There's no doubt about it: you'd be much better off at his place. In restful surroundings you'd soon pull up."

She didn't dare look him in the face, and it didn't take him a second to see what she was driving at.

"You too!" he muttered.

"What do you mean?"

"You think I've made a mistake. You think I'll only make a hash of things and get into trouble over it."

He spoke somewhat heatedly, and the effort brought sweat to his forehead and upper lip.

"Now, now! Keep calm. The doctor will be here in a minute."

He hadn't appeared the previous evening, so Maigret had not seen him since he'd come to collect his wife. The prospect of seeing him again banished for the moment all other preoccupations.

"You'll leave me alone with him."

"And we'll go to Leduc's, shan't we?"

"No, we won't . . . There's his car now. Leave now."

As a rule, Rivaud took the stairs three at a time and strode into his patient's bedroom. Today he mounted step-by-step and came in rather stiffly, though he bowed quite graciously to Madame Maigret as she left the room. Coming over toward Maigret, he put his bag down on the bedside table without so much as a word.

The routine in the morning was always the same. He would put the thermometer under Maigret's tongue and then start undoing the bandages.

That was the situation this morning when the conversation started.

"As a matter of course," began the doctor, "nothing could affect my attitude to a patient. I'll give you exactly the same attention as before. Only, from now on, I should like our relations to end there. And, considering you have no official status here, I forbid you to bother my family anymore."

It wasn't difficult to guess that the speech had been prepared beforehand. Maigret didn't flinch. He was naked from the waist up. The doctor took the thermometer out of his mouth, and muttered:

"A hundred point two."

It was high. He knew it. Rivaud frowned and, without looking at his patient, went on:

"If it hadn't been for yesterday, I should have no hesitation in telling you to go and finish your cure in some quiet country place. But if I tell you so now, it's liable to be misconstrued . . . Am I hurting you?"

He was probing the wound as he spoke.

"No. Go on."

But Rivaud had nothing more to say, and not another word was spoken. He bandaged Maigret up again, put his things away, and washed his hands. At the door, however, he turned and looked the detective in the face.

A difficult look to interpret. Difficult even to say what side of the man was uppermost. Was it the surgeon, the husband of the enigmatic Madame Rivaud, or the brother-in-law of Françoise?

Only one thing was certain. It was a worried look. For a moment he seemed on the point of saying something, but he thought better of it and went out into the passage, where a whispered conversation took place between him and Madame Maigret.

The trouble was that Maigret could now remember his dream perfectly. Was it a bad omen? There certainly were others. When his wound was dressed, for instance, it had hurt much more than on the last two days, though he hadn't admitted it. Another bad sign was that persistent temperature.

He reached for his pipe on the bedside table, but then put it down again.

His wife came in heaving a sigh.

"What did he say?"

"He didn't want to say anything. But I plied him with questions, and he finally told me he had advised you to have a complete rest."

"Quite so. And now tell me how the case is proceeding."

Madame Maigret sat down with an air of resignation, though every line of her body expressed disapproval and misgiving. She deplored his obstinacy and doubted his judgment.

"The postmortem?"

"As near as they can tell the man must have died soon after shooting you."

"They haven't found another revolver?"

"No . . . They've no clue to his identity. There's a

photograph of the corpse in the morning papers, as no one can identify him. It's even in the Paris papers."

"Let's see."

She handed him the paper, and it was with a rather queer sensation that he looked at the picture. For, unreasonable though it was, he had the feeling that he was the one person in the world who had known the man.

It's true he'd never seen him properly; but they'd spent a night together. He recalled his companion's troubled sleep—that is, if he'd slept at all—his deep sighs, and those sounds that Maigret had taken for sobs . . .

And the two legs hanging down from the upper couchette, the patent-leather boots, the thick gray socks . . .

The photograph was horrible, like all police photographs of corpses, touched up as they are to make them look more like a living person and thus facilitate identification.

A dull face. Glassy eyes. And Maigret was not surprised to see a gray beard. Why had he always thought of him with a beard? Even in the railway carriage he had never pictured him otherwise.

And a beard he had, or at least an inch or so of stubble all over his face.

"All the same, this case is no business of yours."

Madame Maigret was at him again, though she spoke very gently and apologetically. She was genuinely concerned about his condition. By the way she looked at him, you'd have thought he was seriously ill.

"At dinner last night I was listening to what the people

were saying. One and all, they're against you. You could question them till you're blue in the face, you wouldn't get a thing out of them. And if that's the case, surely . . ."

"Get a pen and paper, will you?"

He dictated a telegram to a friend of his who was now in the Algiers police:

Urgent please cable Bergerac information Dr. Rivaud at Algiers hospital five years ago greetings thanks.

Madame Maigret's face spoke volumes. She did whatever he asked, but she had no faith in this investigation.

He was conscious of the fact and it infuriated him. Skepticism in other people did not offend him, but in her it was intolerable.

"I'm not asking your advice," he said bitingly as the blood mounted to his cheeks. "All I ask you to do is send off this telegram and bring me any information you hear. You can leave the rest to me."

She threw him a contrite look, but he was too angry to respond.

"From now on, you can keep your thoughts to yourself. In other words, you needn't go shaking your head over me when you talk to Leduc or the doctor or any other of those precious fools."

He turned over onto his side, but so clumsily that once more his mind went back to the seal floundering in the sand.

He was using his left hand, which made his writing heavier and clumsier than usual. He breathed uneasily, being in an uncomfortable position. Two boys were playing marbles under his window, and half a dozen times he nearly shouted out to them to shut up.

> *1st Crime: The daughter-in-law of the farmer at*
> *Moulin-Neuf strangled on the high road.*
> *Long needle driven through heart.*

Maigret sighed and added.

> *(Time? Exact spot? How strong was the victim?)*

And he sighed again to think how quickly, in the ordinary way, he'd have had such questions answered. Running a case from a sickbed was indeed a laborious business. But he plodded on.

> *2nd Crime: Stationmaster's daughter assaulted,*
> *strangled, and has her heart pierced with a*
> *needle.*
> *3rd Crime (abortive): Rosalie attacked.*
> *Aggressor routed. Fiancé says she dreams and*
> *reads novels.*
> *4th Crime: Man jumps out of train as it starts*
> *slowing down before the station. Shoots me*
> *when I follow. Note that this takes place in*

> *the Moulin-Neuf Wood, like the three other*
> *incidents.*
> *5th Crime: The man shot through the brain, in*
> *the same wood.*
> *6th Crime (doubtful): Françoise assaulted in*
> *Moulin-Neuf Wood. Gets the better of the*
> *aggressor.*

He crumpled up the sheet of paper, and with a shrug of his shoulders threw it into a corner. Then he took another and began again.

> *Possibly mad:*
> *Duhourceau?*
> *Rivaud?*
> *Françoise?*
> *Madame Rivaud?*
> *Rosalie?*
> *Inspector?*
> *Landlord?*
> *Leduc?*
> *Man in the train?*

But why was there any need for a lunatic in the story? Maigret frowned suddenly, thinking back to his first few hours in Bergerac. Who was it who had spoken of a madman? Who had suggested that the two crimes could only have been committed by a madman?

Doctor Rivaud!

And who had concurred immediately, who had pointed the official investigation in this direction?

Public Prosecutor Duhourceau!

Suppose one dropped the madman out of the picture? Suppose there was some other logical explanation for this chain of events?

That needle, for instance. Couldn't it have been introduced for no other purpose than to make people think it was a madman or a sadist, at any rate somebody with an unbalanced mind?

Maigret took another sheet, and in capital letters wrote: QUESTIONS. He tried to ornament the letters with fancy squiggles, like a schoolboy dawdling over his work.

1. *Was Rosalie really assaulted or did she only imagine it?*
2. *Was Françoise really assaulted?*
3. *If they were, was it by the same man who murdered the first two?*
4. *Is the man in the train the murderer?*
5. *Who murdered the murderer?*

Madame Maigret returned as he was slowly wading through the last words. She merely glanced at the bed, took off her coat and hat, and sat down beside him.

"Here! I can do that for you," she sighed, mechanically taking the pencil and paper from his hands.

He was at a loss to know how to interpret the gesture. Was she returning to the charge? Or, on the contrary, was she trying to make it up? He couldn't make up his mind whether to flare up again or to melt.

He turned his head away, feeling awkward, as he always did in these situations, while she glanced through what he had written.

"Have you any idea?" she asked gently.

"Not the ghost of one!"

He spoke the words savagely. And they were no more than the truth. He hadn't the ghost of an idea. In fact, he would really have liked to do just what they all wanted him to do—chuck the thing up altogether and go and have a real holiday at Leduc's, where, among the clucking of hens and other nice country noises, he could forget all about being a detective . . .

But he wasn't going to walk back. He wasn't going to take advice from anybody . . .

Did she understand at last? Was she really going to help him instead of stupidly urging him to take it easy? . . . Those were the questions that his troubled eyes were asking.

And she answered with a word she rarely used:

"My poor Maigret!"

For she only called him Maigret on rather special occasions. It implied recognition of his superiority as the man, the mastermind and head of the house. Her tone this time was not one of great conviction, perhaps. But he wasn't out to cavil. He was simply dying for a few crumbs of consolation and encouragement.

"Shove another pillow under my back, will you?"

There! It was all over! No more silly flare-ups, sulks, and makings-up.

"And now the pipe, please."

The two boys below were quarreling now, and one of them got his face slapped and went off to a low house across the square, where he started crying as soon as he found his mother.

"What we need is a plan of action. I think the best thing is to proceed as if we won't receive any new information. In other words, build on what we know already and try out every hypothesis until one of them rings true . . ."

"I met Leduc in the street."

"Did he speak to you?"

"Of course," she answered, smiling. "He once more begged me to use all my influence to induce you to go to La Ribaudière. He had just left the prosecutor's."

"Oh!"

"He rattled on rather volubly, like a man trying to cover his embarrassment."

"Did you go to the mortuary to have another look at the body?"

"There's no mortuary here. It's lying at the police station. There was a queue of at least fifty people lined up to see it. I had to wait my turn."

"You noticed the socks?"

"They're of good wool and certainly hand-knitted."

"Which goes to show the man had some sort of domestic background—a wife, a sister, or a daughter to look after him. Unless he was a tramp. They often get hand-knitted socks from charities, knitted by young ladies of good family."

"Only tramps don't travel second-class—if they go by train at all."

"For that matter, there aren't so many people who do go second-class. A second-class couchette suggests someone who travels a lot. What about the boots?"

"The police looked for a trademark. They found the name of a firm that has branches all over the country."

"And the suit?"

"Of very good black cloth, but it was worn almost threadbare in places. I should think he'd had it quite three years. The overcoat too."

"A hat?"

"They didn't find one. The wind may have blown it away."

Maigret tried to remember whether he had seen the man in a hat. He couldn't be sure.

"Did you notice anything else?"

"The police told me the shirt was mended at the neck and both cuffs. Neatly done, they said."

"The domestic background again . . . And now, what did they find in his pockets? Wallet, papers, bits and pieces?"

"Absolutely nothing except a short ivory cigarette holder."

They were talking it over like two partners, as naturally as could be. Both were relieved that hostilities were over. Maigret puffed away contentedly at his pipe.

"Here's Leduc."

They watched him cross the place du Marché. His hat was tipped slightly backward and he walked with almost a slouch. When he came into the room, he was too preoccupied even to greet Madame Maigret.

"I've been seeing the prosecutor."

"I know."

"Yes, of course . . . We met in the street . . . Then I went to the police station to make sure it was true—what he told me . . . It's simply bewildering . . . ?"

"Let's hear it."

Leduc mopped his forehead and drank half the glass of lemonade that had been prepared for Maigret.

"You don't mind, do you? . . . I've never been so flabbergasted in my life . . . They sent the fingerprints to Paris, as a matter of course . . . Well, the answer's just come."

"Go on."

"The man whom you jumped out of the train after died years ago."

"What are you talking about?"

"I say that officially this corpse that's lying at the police station has been a corpse for years. He was a man called Meyer—though known by the name of Samuel—who was condemned to death at Algiers, and . . ."

Maigret was leaning forward in the bed.

"And executed?"

"No. He died in the hospital a few days before."

Madame Maigret couldn't help smiling maternally as she watched the glow of happiness that spread over her husband's face. He noticed it and nearly smiled back, but dignity got the upper hand and he kept a grave face.

"And what had he done, this Samuel?"

"We don't know. It was only a short telegram in code, but it said further particulars would follow. We ought to hear by this evening . . . Of course they may be making a mistake. And there's always the chance of two men's fingerprints being alike. One in a hundred thousand—isn't that what Bertillon says? It is possible this is one of those cases."

"And how is Duhourceau taking the blow?"

"He's annoyed, naturally. Thinks he may have to call in outside help. But he's afraid they might send chaps who'd take their orders from you. That's what he wanted to see me about. Wanted to know whether you had a lot of influence at headquarters."

"Fill me another pipe," said Maigret to his wife.

"That's the third."

"Never mind. I'll bet anything you like my temperature's right down to normal . . . Samuel. Meyer. Sounds Jewish to me. The family counts a lot with the Jews, so we needn't be surprised he wore hand-knitted socks. They're thrifty too, which can explain why a man who could afford a second-class sleeper should wear a threadbare suit . . ."

He interrupted himself:

"Don't mind me. I don't mind telling you I've had a wretched few hours. Nothing in my head but that dream. But now the seal—that is, if it is a seal and not a whale—is on the move again. And just you watch him go!"

He burst out laughing at the look of pained bewilderment on Leduc's face.

SAMUEL

The same evening brought news from two sources. The time for the doctor's visit was approaching when a telegram arrived from Algiers.

> Doctor Rivaud unknown all hospitals here greetings Martin

Maigret had hardly glanced at it when Leduc appeared. The telegram caught his eye at once, but he asked no questions. Maigret, however, held it out to him.

"Have a look at this."

Leduc read it.

"What can you expect?"

He shrugged his shoulders, and though he said no more, his whole attitude expressed what he was thinking:

"It's no use hoping to understand anything in this case. Every day brings further complications, and if you had a grain of sense you'd let me take you off to La Ribaudière."

Madame Maigret was out. In spite of the gathering twilight, Maigret did not think of switching on the light.

The streetlamps were lit, and he liked to look out at the ring of lights that encircled the place du Marché, and the windows of the houses as they lit up one by one. The first was always the same, a window in the second house to the left of the garage; and, by the lamp inside, the same dressmaker was always sitting in the same position, bending over her work.

"The police have had news too," grunted Leduc.

He said it reluctantly. He didn't want Maigret to think he was ready to help him. Or perhaps the police had asked him not to pass on any information to the enemy.

"News of Samuel?"

"Yes. The particulars came by the afternoon post. And then Lucas telephoned from Paris. He'd had his eye on the man at one time, though it's several years ago now."

"What do they say?"

"They don't know exactly where he came from. But they think he was born in Poland, possibly Yugoslavia. An uncommunicative man who never talked about himself. He had a business in Algiers. Guess what."

"Something very dull, I should imagine."

"Postage stamps."

Maigret was delighted. Dealing in stamps seemed to him somehow just right for the man in the train.

"A business that naturally was only cover for another. But it was so well done that, though the police were watching them, they didn't find out anything till Samuel was put on trial for murder. Then it all came to light. I'm more or less repeating what Lucas told me over the phone. His real business was supplying forged passports, immigration papers, and labor permits. He had a whole network of agents in Bucharest, Warsaw, Constantinople, and all over the shop."

The sky outside was a deep dark blue, the tops of the houses barely visible against it. From down below came the familiar buzz of the aperitif hour.

"Strange," muttered Maigret.

What he found strange was not Samuel's profession, but to find in a place like Bergerac links extending from Warsaw to Algiers.

People like this Samuel—he had dealt with hundreds in his time. And he had always studied them with curiosity that was mixed with some other feeling—not quite repulsion—as though they belonged to a different species altogether from the one we call human.

You'd find them as barmen in Scandinavia, as gangsters in America, as casino owners in Holland, or else as headwaiters or theater directors in Germany, or wholesalers in North Africa.

And now they were cropping up again in this peaceful little town of Bergerac, which you would have taken for the most remote place imaginable from all the terror, sordidness, and tragedy that their doings involved.

Eastern and Central Europe between Budapest and Odessa, between Tallinn and Belgrade, an area teeming with a mass of humanity. In particular, there were hundreds of thousands of hungry Jews whose only ambition was to seek a better existence in some other land. Boatloads and trainloads of emigrants with children in their arms, and dragging their old folk behind them, resigned, tragic faces queuing at border checkpoints.

There were more Poles in Chicago than Americans . . . France alone had absorbed trainloads and trainloads. In every town in the country there were people who at every birth, death, or marriage had to spell their outlandish names letter by letter at the town hall . . .

Some were legal emigrants, with their papers in order. Others didn't have the patience to wait, or were unable to obtain a visa.

That's where Samuel came in, Samuel and his like. Men who spoke ten languages, who knew every frontier in Europe, the rubber stamp of every consulate, and even the signatures of the officials. They could see to everything!

Their real activity would be concealed behind the façade of some other business, preferably international.

Postage stamps. What could be better?

To Mr A. Levy, Chicago.
Sir,
I am this day dispatching two hundred
rare Czechoslovakian stamps with orange
vignettes . . .

There was another traffic, too, which no doubt interested Samuel, as it did most of his kind.

In the *maisons spéciales* of South America it was

French girls who formed the quality. Their purveyors worked in Paris on the Grands Boulevards. But the smaller fry, the cheaper end of the market, came from Eastern Europe. Country girls who left home at fifteen or sixteen, returning—if ever they did—at twenty, with their dowries in their pockets.

What bothered Maigret was the sudden irruption of this Samuel into the world of Bergerac, where previously there had been only the public prosecutor, the doctor and his wife, Françoise, Leduc, and the hotel proprietor to deal with. It cast a whole new complexion on the case.

Opposite, Maigret could see the little grocer's, whose wares he had come to know so well. And then the garage with its petrol pump—which must have been for show, for they only ever sold petrol in cans!

But Leduc was speaking.

"I never heard of a show of that kind run from Algiers, but they say he did a lot of business with the Arabs, and even with the Negroes inland."

"There was a murder, you said?"

"A double one. Two of his own race who were found lying dead on a bit of waste ground. Both had come from Berlin. There was a lot of nosing around. It was discovered that the two men had been working with Samuel for a long time. The investigation lasted for months. They found nothing. Samuel was taken ill and had to be moved from the prison infirmary to the town hospital.

"They more or less pieced it all together. The two associates from Berlin had come to complain of something. No doubt he was doing them out of their commissions. Perhaps they threatened him."

"So he did away with them."

"He was condemned to death. But there was no need to carry out the execution, for he died in the hospital a few days after being sentenced.

"That's all I know."

———

The doctor was astonished to find the two men in the dark. With a curt movement he switched on the light. Then he put his dispatch case down on the table, nodded a good evening, slipped off his light overcoat, and started washing his hands in the basin.

"I'll leave you now," said Leduc. "See you again tomorrow."

He hadn't realized the doctor would be coming, and was none too pleased at being found there. It was all very well for Maigret, but Leduc lived in the district. He didn't want to rub people the wrong way.

"Look after yourself. Good-bye, doctor," he said, slinking out.

Rivaud merely grunted as he soaped his hands.

"How's the temperature?"

"Behaving very nicely."

Maigret was in the same buoyant good humor now

as he had been during the first few days, when it had felt so good to be alive.

"Does it still hurt?"

"Oh, that's nothing. I'm used to it by now."

Once more the doctor went through the routine: unbandaging, dressing, rebandaging. His face was within a foot or two of Maigret's. And suddenly the latter blurted out:

"One would hardly take you for a Jew."

No response. Not a flicker. Not the faintest variation in the surgeon's regular breathing. Only after the job was finished did he say:

"It's safe to move you now."

"What do you mean?"

"You need no longer be a prisoner in this hotel room. Wasn't there talk of your spending a few days with Leduc?"

A man of prodigious self-control, if ever there was one! For a good quarter of an hour Maigret had been fixing him with a steady stare, and he hadn't turned a hair. His careful capable hands had never trembled, never faltered.

"I'll only be coming every other day now. The other days I'll send my assistant. You can have every confidence in him."

"As much as in you?"

There were moments—though they could hardly be called frequent—when Maigret could not repress a pert remark like that. But what really gave them their flavor was the artless way in which they were said.

"Good evening!"

That was all he got for an answer. The doctor was gone, leaving Maigret to resume his mental puppet show. And now Samuel, who had just been added to his collection, had now stepped forward to play the principal part. A man who had the rare distinction of having died twice.

Was he the man who went about strangling women? Was he the man who had a mania for sticking needles through hearts?

If he was, there were several questions that were hard to answer, two in particular.

First of all, why should he choose the neighborhood of Bergerac for the scene of his activities? People of his sort invariably preferred big towns, where the inhabitants were more mixed and where, as a result, there was a greater chance of passing unnoticed . . .

And apparently he had no connection with Bergerac at all. At least, nobody had been able to identify him. Moreover, with those patent-leather boots, he hardly seemed cast for the part of wild man of the woods.

If he didn't live in the woods, where did he hang out? Was somebody hiding him? Who could it be? The doctor perhaps? Leduc? Duhourceau? The Hôtel d' Angleterre.

Secondly, the crimes in Algiers had been clever, premeditated murders with a purpose—to get rid of two dangerous accomplices.

The Bergerac murders, on the other hand, were committed by a madman, a sadist, or a sexual pervert.

Had Samuel gone mad between the earlier and the later crimes? Or, for some subtle reason, was he feigning madness, using the needle as some sort of cover?

"I wonder if Duhourceau's ever been to Algiers . . . !" muttered Maigret to himself.

His wife returned. She was tired out. Throwing her hat on to the table, she sank into the easy chair.

"What a trade! I'm sorry for you. To have to prowl around like that from one year's end to the other!"

"Any news?"

"Nothing interesting. Nobody's yet been able to identify the dead man. It seems they've had some information from Paris, but they won't give it out."

"I know it."

"Leduc told you? That's nice of him. One couldn't blame him if he washed his hands of you. Everybody's against you. Now people don't know what to think. Some say that Samuel has nothing to do with it at all. He's just a man who wanted to kill himself. And naturally they're expecting the murders to go on."

"Have you been past the doctor's house again?"

"Yes, but there was nothing to see. On the other hand, I was told something, though it may be of no importance at all. Two or three times a woman has visited the house, and she's thought to be Dr. Rivaud's mother-in-law. A middle-aged woman, they say, and decidedly common. Nobody knows anything about her or where she lives, and she hasn't been seen for quite two years . . ."

"Hand me the telephone."

He rang up the police station.

"Is that the inspector's secretary? . . . No. No need to bother him . . . I only want to know the surname of Mademoiselle Françoise, Madame Rivaud's sister. No objection, have you?"

A few moments later, he smiled. With his hand over the receiver, he said to his wife:

"They're calling the inspector to see if it is all right to give me the information. He'd have liked not to tell me. They hate the idea of helping me even that much! . . . Hello . . . yes . . . Beausoleil? . . . Thank you.

"A splendid name! And now there's a very boring job for you to do. I want you to go downstairs and ask for the telephone directory—not the local one, but the big one for the whole of France. Look up the numbers of every medical school in the country and then telephone to each in turn. Ask for the registrar's office, and inquire whether anyone of the name of Jacques Rivaud is on their list of qualified men . . ."

"You think he might not be . . . But he's the person who is taking care of you . . ."

"Just do it."

"You want me to phone from the kiosk in the lounge? People can hear every word you say."

"Splendid."

Left alone, again, he filled his pipe and closed the window, for it had turned a little chilly.

He had always loved the atmosphere of a house, and it fascinated him to speculate on that of the doctor's and the prosecutor's. There was certainly something haunting about the doctor's.

Not on the surface. In fact, quite the opposite. A gay little villa with clean, simple lines, plainly decorated.

"They must be a happy household . . ."

That's what the passersby must say as they saw the well-lit rooms, the brightly colored curtains, the flowers in the garden, the brightly polished brass knocker, and the car purring in the front of the garage . . . And that supple, graceful girl, Françoise, jumping in and driving off . . . Or it might be Rivaud, who, with his forceful, capable look, cut as good a figure as she did . . .

What would they say to each other in the evenings, those three?

Was Madame Rivaud aware of what was going on between her husband and her sister?

She wasn't pretty. And certainly she knew it. Nothing romantic or exciting about her. More like the resigned, long-suffering mother of a family . . .

Françoise, on the other hand, was simply overflowing with life . . . Yes, it was an interesting question—whether Madame Rivaud knew. Would she meekly accept it? It often happened. Maigret had come across such situations time and again, even in the most respectable families . . .

Or were there, on the contrary, a lot of lies and false pretenses? Secret meetings ... Kisses behind doors ...

What sort of people were these Beausoleils? And was this story about the hospital in Algiers true? ... Common. That's what was said of the mother. And even Madame Rivaud—there were little things that, if you looked closely, hinted at a humbler origin. She had never quite been able to pick up the step. Françoise was more intelligent, more adaptable ... And, of course, she'd started younger. She could pass herself off anywhere.

Were they jealous of each other? Did they hate each other? Or would they have long heart-to-heart talks?

And their mother, who had come to Bergerac on two occasions ... Maigret couldn't help picturing her as a stout busybody, delighted at having got her daughters settled, and lecturing them on how nice they ought to be to so rich and important a gentleman as Dr. Rivaud.

Perhaps the rich gentleman paid her a small annuity.

"I can picture her in Paris, in the eighteenth arrondissement, or rather in Nice ..."

Did they talk about the crimes over dinner?

But there was a limit after all what could be imagined. If only he had been able to drop in and have a look! Even for five minutes. To see the rooms, the ornaments, the things left lying about, which told of the daily occupations of those who lived in them ...

Duhourceau's house too. He would have given a good deal for five minutes there. Certainly there was some connection between Duhourceau and the doctor. You could tell it by their attitudes. There was some sort of an alliance . . .

Abruptly Maigret rang the bell and asked the landlord to come up. As soon as the man appeared, he asked him bluntly:

"Do you know if Monsieur Duhourceau often dines at the Rivauds'?"

"Every Tuesday. I know very well because it's my nephew who drives him in his taxi. You see . . ."

"Thank you."

"Is that all?"

"That's all."

The landlord went off, puzzled, while Maigret, returning to the doctor's villa, spread a clean white cloth and laid the table for four . . . The public prosecutor would sit on Madame Rivaud's right . . .

"Tuesday night! . . . And it was a Tuesday night—or rather early Wednesday morning—that I was attacked and Samuel was killed."

So they were having dinner together that night. With the feeling that he was making a huge stride forward, he grabbed the phone.

"Hallo! . . . Is that the exchange? . . . Police Judiciaire . . ."

He spoke almost roughly, for he was afraid he might get the brush-off.

"I want to know if Dr. Rivaud received a call from Paris last Tuesday."

"Hold on, will you? I'll find out."

It didn't take a minute.

"Yes. At two in the afternoon. A call from Paris. The number calling was Archives 14–67."

"Have you a numeral list of Paris subscribers? If you have, I'd like to know who Archives 14–67 is."

"I think I've seen one. Hold on again."

A nice girl. Pretty too, by the sound of her voice. And gay. Maigret smiled unconsciously.

"Hallo! . . . I've found it. It's the Restaurant des Quatres Sergents, place de la Bastille."

"Was it a three-minute call?"

"Three units. Nine minutes altogether."

A nine-minute call at two o'clock. The train left at three. That evening, while Maigret was lying beneath his sleepless, tormented companion in that overheated compartment, the public prosecutor was having dinner with the Rivauds . . .

Maigret fumed with impatience. It was all he could do not to jump out of bed. He felt he was getting on the trail at last. It was no longer time for leisurely musings. He mustn't make a mistake now.

The truth was not far off. Very likely he had all the data he needed. It might be simply a question of seeing it clearly in its right perspective. But it was precisely at such moments as this that there was the greatest risk of dashing off on a wild-goose chase.

Let's see. A table laid for four. Monsieur Duhourceau—why was it Rosalie had looked at him like

that? Had he a bad name in the town? Was there a side
of his life that ill accorded with his age and the dignity
of his position? In a country town it was easy enough to
get a bad name. You only had to pat a girl on the cheek
to set tongues wagging . . .

And Françoise? . . . The type that made men of a
certain age start thinking of things they shouldn't . . .
So they are at dinner and Samuel and I are on the train.
Was Samuel afraid? Wasn't that the most obvious explanation of his restlessness, his trembling hands, his
breathing?

Maigret was sweating. From downstairs came the
clatter of plates. It would soon be dinnertime.

*"Did he jump out of the train to escape from some-
body or to meet somebody?"*

That was perhaps the most crucial question of all. In
fact, Maigret felt pretty sure it was. If he could answer
that, it would take him a long way. Once more he repeated:

*"Was it to escape from somebody or to meet some-
body?* Which did the telephone call suggest?"

His wife entered, so flustered herself that she did not
notice the state of excitement to which Maigret had
worked himself up.

"We must call in another doctor at once. A real
one . . . It's simply monstrous. It's a crime . . . And to
think . . ."

She looked at her husband as though to make sure
he was safe and sound.

"No one's ever qualified under the name of Jacques Rivaud. He simply isn't a doctor! . . . Every register has been searched . . . And now we're getting to the bottom of it—that temperature of yours that wouldn't go down. Of course the wound wouldn't heal! . . ."

"I know," said Maigret to himself triumphantly. "I'm sure of it. *It was to meet somebody.*"

The telephone rang. The landlord's voice saying:

"Monsieur Duhourceau asks if he can come up."

8

A COLLECTOR OF BOOKS

The minute that elapsed before the prosecutor appeared saw a complete change in Maigret's features. His face became dull and resigned, like that of any other invalid who is sick to death of lying in bed.

This change in his expression seemed even to affect the room. It too looked dull. A commonplace and dreary hotel bedroom, devoid of personality. It wasn't even tidy. The bed had not been made since the morning, the bedside table was cluttered with medicine, glasses, and spoons, and Madame Maigret's hat was still lying where she had thrown it down on the table.

The latter had just lit the spirit lamp to make an infusion, and that didn't add to the dignity of the room either. One could hardly say it looked sordid: yet it was not far off.

Two or three sharp little knocks on the door. Madame Maigret opened it, and once again the prosecutor unthinkingly handed her his hat and stick.

"Good evening, inspector," he said, coming toward the bed.

He didn't seem embarrassed. On the contrary, his

manner was more like that of a man who has pulled himself thoroughly together to accomplish some task.

"Good evening, *monsieur le procureur*. Won't you sit down?"

For the first time, Maigret noticed a smile on the prosecutor's forbidding face. Just a little one at the corners of the mouth. It had, of course, been put there on purpose.

"I must confess I've been feeling a bit guilty about you . . . That surprises you, does it? . . . I couldn't help reproaching myself for having been rather curt with you . . . Though you must admit that your own manner is sometimes rather—disconcerting . . ."

Sitting with both hands spread out on his knees, he leant forward toward Maigret, who stared back at him with bovine eyes, devoid of thought.

"So I thought I'd look in to let you know how we were getting on . . ."

Certainly Maigret was listening, but he would have been hard put to it to repeat a single word of what was said to him. What he was really concentrating on was the face in front of him, which he studied detail by detail.

A very fair complexion, almost too fair, set off by the gray hair . . . Monsieur Duhourceau was certainly not troubled by his liver. Nor was he either gouty or apoplectic . . .

What would be the weak spot in his constitution? For after all you didn't reach the age of sixty-five without having a weak spot.

"Arteriosclerosis," answered Maigret to himself.

And he glanced at the thin fingers, the hands with their silky skin, the veins standing out and looking as hard as glass . . .

A small man, dry, highly strung, intelligent, and irascible.

"And morally? Isn't there a weak spot there too?"

Of course there was. For in spite of all the prosecutor's dignity and arrogance, there was something vague, evasive, and shamefaced about him.

Meanwhile he was talking:

"In two or three days at the outside we'll have the case finished and filed. The facts speak for themselves . . . We must keep to the point. How Samuel dodged execution and had somebody else buried in his place—that's for the Algiers people to go into. That is, if they think it worthwhile . . . I don't for a moment suppose they will . . ."

There were moments when his voice wavered ever so slightly. They were when he looked into Maigret's eyes for some response, only to come up against that empty, bovine stare. He didn't know quite how to take it. Was the inspector listening? Was he being ironical?

Clearing his voice, he went on:

"Anyhow, this Samuel, who may have been none too sane in Africa, escapes and comes to France, where he definitely becomes insane. There are plenty of indications. It's a type of case that's frequently met with, as Dr. Rivaud will tell you. In the course of his fits of ma-

nia he commits the two murders. In the train he thinks
you are after him. He fires at you and brings you down,
but finally, in a fit of madness, he shoots himself . . ."

With an airy sweep of the hand, he added:

"The fact that no revolver was found by his side
doesn't bother me in the least. There are dozens of cases
on record in which the same thing's happened. Somebody has passed and picked it up—a vagrant perhaps,
or a child—and never said a word about it. Too scared to
come forward. Sometimes it's ten or twenty years afterward that the whole story comes to light . . . The important thing in this case was to make sure the gun was fired
close to the head. The postmortem leaves no doubt on
that point. There, in a few words, you have . . ."

Maigret for his part was asking himself:

"What is his vice?"

Not drink. Not gambling. And strangely enough,
Maigret was tempted to add: not women.

Avarice? That seemed much nearer the mark. It
needed no effort at all to picture Monsieur Duhourceau,
having locked every door, opening the safe and laying
its contents out on the table—bundles of notes, bags of
gold coins, bonds . . .

All in all, he gave the impression of a solitary person.
Gambling is a sociable vice, women too. So is drink,
nearly always . . .

"Have you ever been in Algiers, Monsieur Duhourceau?"

"Me?"

When a man says "me" like that, you can bet your boots he's trying to gain time.

"Why do you ask me that? Do I look like a colonial? No, I've never set foot in Algiers. In fact, I've never crossed the Mediterranean. My longest journey was a trip to the Norwegian fjords. That was in 1923 . . ."

"Of course . . . I really don't know what made me ask the question. Stupid of me. Perhaps it's this wound of mine. You've no idea how much it's run me down . . ."

It was an old trick of Maigret's to rattle along unconcernedly, jumping abruptly from one subject to another. His listener would suspect a trap, and, making a great effort not to give anything away, would end by getting all hot and bothered and losing the thread of his own ideas.

"It's left me pretty weak. That's what I was saying to the doctor. By the way, who does the cooking at their place?"

"The . . . ?"

Maigret didn't give him time to reply.

"If it's one of the two sisters, it's certainly not Françoise. It's easier to see her driving a high-powered car than standing over the kitchen range stirring a soup . . . Would you mind passing me that glass of water?"

Maigret raised himself on an elbow and drank from the glass, but so clumsily that he dropped it and spilt the contents over Monsieur Duhourceau's legs.

"I'm so sorry. I really don't know what's the matter with me. Fortunately it won't leave a mark." And turning to his wife: "Bring a cloth, will you?"

Monsieur Duhourceau was furious. The water had gone right through his trousers and must be trickling down his calf.

"Don't bother, madame," he said, pulling out his handkerchief. "As you husband says, it won't leave a mark. So it doesn't matter in the least."

The words were charged with sarcasm.

This little incident, coming on top of Maigret's none too tactful ramblings, had put the prosecutor thoroughly out of countenance. The engaging manner he had adopted at the start had completely evaporated.

He was standing now, but he did not go, as he had not yet said all he had come to say. With an effort he regained his self-possession, but there was precious little cordiality in his voice as he asked:

"For your part, inspector, what are your intentions?"

"The same as ever."

"You mean . . . ?"

"To arrest the murderer, of course. And after that . . . Well, if there's any time left, I'll have a peep at that La Ribaudière, where I ought to have been spending this last week or more."

Monsieur Duhourceau went white with rage. What? He had taken the trouble to pay this friendly call, to explain things patiently. He had been treating Maigret almost deferentially.

And the latter had first poured a glass of water down his legs—and what's more, done it on purpose (the prosecutor felt sure of that)—and then had the cheek to say:

"I'll arrest the murderer."

Yes, that's what he'd said to him, to him, the public prosecutor, who had taken infinite pains to explain that there was no longer anybody to arrest. It sounded almost like a threat. The only thing to do now was to walk out and slam the door.

But Monsieur Duhourceau didn't. In fact, he even mustered some sort of a smile.

"You're very obstinate, inspector."

"Oh, you know . . . When you're lying in bed all day with nothing to do . . . By the way, I wonder if you'd have any books to lend me?"

Still jumping from subject to subject. Still putting out feelers. And this time he thought he saw a flicker of anxiety trouble the prosecutor's eye.

"I'll send you some."

"Amusing ones. Nothing too serious."

"I must be going now."

"My wife will give you your hat and stick. Are you dining at home?"

Maigret held out his hand, and the prosecutor had to shake it. The door shut, while Maigret lay back against his pillows, looking thoughtfully at the ceiling.

"Do you really think . . . ?" began his wife.

"Is Rosalie still working in the hotel?"

"So far as I know. In fact, I think it was her I saw on the stairs just now."

"Fetch her."

"People will say . . ."

"Never mind if they do."

While waiting for the maid, Maigret thought to himself:

"Duhourceau's afraid. He's been afraid all along. Afraid I'll discover the criminal. Afraid I'll delve into his private life. Rivaud's afraid too. So's his wife."

What did they fear? And what had they to do with Samuel, the dealer in forged papers and wretched girls from Eastern Europe?

The prosecutor was not a Jew. Rivaud could quite well be one, though it was by no means certain.

The door opened, and Rosalie, wiping her big red hands on her coarse linen apron, was led into the room by Madame Maigret.

"You wanted to see me?"

"Yes. Come in and sit down."

"We're not allowed to sit down in the visitors' rooms."

The way in which she said it warned Maigret of a change. She was no longer the familiar chatterbox. She'd obviously had a ticking-off, perhaps she had even been threatened.

"I only wanted to ask you a simple question. Have you ever worked at Monsieur Duhourceau's?"

"I was two years with him."

"I thought you might have been. As cook or housemaid?"

"Housemaid."

"You went all over the house, polishing the floors, and dusting . . . ?"

"I did the rooms . . ."

"Exactly. You did the rooms. And in doing the rooms you must have found out a thing or two. How long ago was it?"

"It's a year last month that I left the place."

"So you were the same pretty girl you are now. Yes, yes, it's no use pretending you're not."

Maigret wasn't laughing. He had an art all of his own of saying things like that quite gravely, in the most convincing manner. As a matter of fact, it wasn't far from the truth, for Rosalie was a pleasant-looking girl. Her buxom figure had certainly attracted many an inquisitive hand.

"Did the prosecutor sometimes watch you at work?"

"What an idea! Perhaps you think I got him to carry my pails for me!"

Rosalie was very scornful, but she softened at once as her eye lit on Madame Maigret, who was pottering about the room, tidying and brushing up the crumbs. She kept her eyes fixed on her, and at last she couldn't help saying:

"I'll bring you a little hand-brush in the morning. There's a spare one downstairs. That broom's such a clumsy thing."

"Did he often have women visitors?"

"I don't know."

"Yes, you do. Come on! Speak out. There's nothing to be frightened of. Don't forget I was on your side yesterday when the others wouldn't believe you."

"It wouldn't do anybody any good."

"What wouldn't?"

"If I did speak out. You see, there's Albert—my fiancé. It would spoil his chances. He's trying to get a government job. Besides, they might shut me up in a madhouse—just because I dream every night and talk about my dreams."

She was working herself up and only needed a little egging on.

"So there was a lady visitor now and again?"

"No, there wasn't."

"Then, perhaps on his trips to Bordeaux."

"I don't care two pins about his trips to Bordeaux."

"Come on, now! There's a little bit of scandal somewhere isn't there?"

"And everybody knows about it . . . You can't keep things dark forever. They've a way of coming out by themselves . . . It was a good two years ago . . . A parcel came from Paris, but when they came to look at it, the label was more than half gone and they couldn't tell who it was for. And there was no sender's name on it either . . .

"They waited a week, thinking someone might turn up to claim it. And then they opened it . . . You'd never guess what they found . . .

"Photographs. But not ordinary ones. Women with no clothes on . . . And not just women alone—couples too.

"As you can imagine, everybody was guessing who

had pictures of that sort sent them from Paris. I think they even called the police in.

"And then, one day, another parcel came, just the same as the first one. Same paper, same string, same label as the bit that had been left before . . . Guess who it was addressed to! . . . Monsieur Duhourceau, if you please."

Maigret was not in the least surprised. Hadn't he already decided that the prosecutor's vice was a solitary one?

So it wasn't to count out his money that the prosecutor would lock his study door at night. In the fine but somber room on the first floor he would sit poring over naughty photographs and forbidden books.

"Listen, Rosalie! Not a word you say here will ever be repeated. And now confess that when you heard what you've just told me, you went and had a look at the books in his study."

"Who told you so? . . . Well, since you know it already, I admit I did . . . A lot of the bookcases have doors to them with a sort of wire netting, and they're always kept locked. Only, I once found one where the key had been left in the lock . . ."

"What did you find?"

"You know very well what I found. It was so awful that I had nightmares for a week and I couldn't endure Albert coming anywhere near me."

Oho! Her relations with the fair young man were no longer a mystery.

"Big books, weren't they? Printed on good paper, with engravings?"

"Yes . . . But they were all sorts . . . Terrible ones. Things you'd never think of . . ."

Was that the sum total of Monsieur Duhourceau's iniquity? If so, it was rather pitiful. A lonely old bachelor who occupied a high position and didn't dare smile at a girl for fear of raising the devil.

And the only consolation he could find was to become a collector in this murky backwater of art, filling his locked bookcases with licentious engravings, erotic photographs, and those books that the catalogues amiably describe as "works for connoisseurs."

No wonder he was afraid.

Only it wasn't easy to see what relation that could have with the two murders—still less with Samuel . . . Unless the latter had also dealt in naughty pictures.

Maigret wondered.

Meanwhile Rosalie stood awkwardly, shifting from one foot to the other, astonished herself at having said so much.

"If your wife hadn't been here I should never have dreamt of talking about such things."

"Did Dr. Rivaud often come to the house?"

"Hardly ever. He used to telephone."

"Nor anyone of his family?"

"No. Except, of course, for Mademoiselle Françoise the time she was acting as his secretary."

"Whose? The prosecutor's?"

"Yes. She brought her typewriter with her—a funny little thing that shut up in a box."

"What did she see to—his professional work?"

"Oh, I wouldn't know anything about that. All I can tell you is that she'd work on one side of the big curtain that ran right across one end of the library and he on the other."

"And?"

"And nothing! Don't you go putting words into my mouth. All the time she was there I never saw a thing you could take exception to."

"How long did it last?"

"Barely six months. After that she went off to her mother's in Paris or Bordeaux, I'm not sure which."

"And Monsieur Duhourceau never overstepped the mark in his dealings with you?"

"He'd have caught it, if he had!"

"Well, Rosalie, thank you for what you've told me. Don't be frightened. You won't get into any trouble over it, and Albert will never know you came."

After shutting the door behind Rosalie, Madame Maigret sighed.

"Oh, dear, oh, dear! To think an educated, intelligent man—and in such a position too . . ."

Madame Maigret was always astonished when she ran into anything that was ugly. It was impossible for her to imagine any more noxious instincts than those of a good wife whose only regret was to have had no children.

"Don't you think that girl exaggerates? If you ask

me, she's out to make herself interesting. She'd say anything for the sake of being listened to. And I wouldn't mind betting she was never attacked at all . . ."

"Nor would I."

"And the same goes for Françoise. She's not strong. A powerful man would get her down with one hand—and yet she says she drove him off."

"You're quite right."

"I'll go farther. If this sort of thing goes on another week, we'll have such a jumble of truth and lies being told that we shan't know whether to believe anybody. These stories work on people's minds, and from thinking things they come to believe they're true . . . There's Monsieur Dohourceau being painted in the most lurid colors. It'll be the police inspector's turn next—they'll be saying he cheats on his wife . . . And as for you, heaven knows what they're saying about you already. It won't be long before I have to stick my marriage lines up on the wall if I'm not to pass for your mistress . . ."

An affectionate smile spread over Maigret's face as he looked at her. She was quite incensed. All these complications were rather upsetting.

"And to crown it all, a doctor who isn't a doctor! . . ."

"Who knows?"

"What do you mean 'who knows'? Haven't I telephoned to every university in France?"

"Could you give me my infusion?"

"That's one thing that won't do you any harm! It's my prescription, not that imposter's."

As he drank, he kept her hand in his. It was warm in the room. A thin plume of steam hissed out of the radiator in a regular rhythm, like a cat purring. Downstairs, dinner was finished, and the guests were starting to play games of billiards and backgammon.

"A good infusion gives a man heart."

"Yes, dear . . . a good infusion."

He kissed her hand, the tenderness of the gesture disguised by his air of irony.

"If all goes well we'll be out of the woods in two or three days."

"And as soon as you are—I know you—you'll only be plunging into another."

9

THE KIDNAPPING OF AN OLD-TIME ARTISTE

It tickled Maigret to see the sulky look that came into Leduc's face.

"What do you want me to do?" grumbled the latter. "What do you mean by a delicate mission?"

"A mission that only you can fulfill. Come on! There's no need to look so glum about it. I'm not going to ask you to burgle the prosecutor's house, nor even Dr. Rivaud's."

Maigret held out a Bordeaux newspaper, pointing to a small advertisement:

A certain Madame Beausoleil, formerly of Algiers, now believed in Bordeaux, is urgently requested to present herself at once at the following address, where she will learn of something to her advantage. Maigret, Notary, Hôtel d' Angleterre, Bergerac.

Leduc did not smile. The sulky expression only deepened.

"And you want me to play the notary?"

His voice expressed such intense distaste that Madame Maigret, at the other end of the room, burst out laughing.

"Oh, no. I'm the notary. The notice is appearing this morning in a dozen papers of the Bordeaux district as well as in the chief Paris dailies."

"Why Bordeaux?"

"Never mind that. How many trains a day arrive from Bordeaux?"

"Three or four, I think. Perhaps more."

"Well, look here! It's a nice bright day. Not too hot. Not too cold. Is there a café opposite the station? Your mission is to go and meet each train as it comes in, until Madame Beausoleil appears."

"I don't know her."

"Nor do I. I couldn't even tell you whether she's tall or short. But I fancy you will be able to spot her all right. She'll be anything from forty-five to sixty, vulgar, and probably showy. The chances are she's stout."

"The advertisement tells her to come to the hotel. So I don't see why I . . ."

"Quite so. Quite so. Only I have an idea there'll be somebody else at the station who'll try to stop the good lady coming. See? Understand the mission? Bring her all the same. Use your winning ways."

Maigret had never seen the station, but lying in front of him was a picture postcard of it. The platform was in a blaze of sun, but even in the shadow you could make out the stationmaster's office and the lamp room.

It tickled Maigret to think of poor Leduc in his straw hat, pacing up and down that sunny platform waiting for the train, then rushing up to elderly ladies to ask them if their name was Beausoleil.

"I'm counting on you."

"Very well . . . Since it's all arranged . . ."

He walked off sorrowfully. He couldn't get his car to start, and had to crank it a long time before it spluttered into action.

A little later Dr. Rivaud's assistant arrived, bowing profusely to Madame Maigret and then to her husband. A ginger-headed young man, shy and bony, who tripped over every piece of furniture and apologized with a running fire of beg-your-pardons and excuse-me's.

"Excuse me! Might I have a little hot water?"

And as he nearly bowled over the bedside table:

"I'm so sorry . . . I beg your pardon . . ."

As he dressed the wound he kept on saying:

"You'll tell me if I'm hurting you . . . Just a moment. Excuse me . . . Could you lift yourself a little higher in the bed? . . . Thank you. Thank you. That's splendid."

Meanwhile Maigret smiled to think of Leduc parking the old Ford outside the station.

"Is Dr. Rivaud very busy?"

"Very busy, yes. He always is."

"A very active man, I dare say."

"Extremely so. In fact he's extraordinary . . . Am I hurting you? . . . Thank you . . . He begins at seven in the morning with the free consultations. Then there's his private clinic. And then the hospital . . . He never leaves anything important to me. Always wants to see to it himself."

"I suppose it's never crossed your mind that he might not be qualified?"

The young man nearly choked, then decided that Maigret was only pulling his leg.

"You're joking . . . My chief is not merely a doctor, he's a great doctor. If he set up in Paris he'd be famous in no time."

The young man was absolutely sincere. His words rang with an admiration that made no reserves.

"Do you know where he qualified?"

"Montpellier, I think. In fact, I'm practically sure. I've heard him speak of the professors there. After that he was in Paris, where he was assistant to Dr. Martel."

"You're sure of that?"

"There's a picture hanging in his consulting room— a photograph of Dr. Martel surrounded by his pupils."

"That's odd."

"I beg your pardon, but did you really think he wasn't qualified?"

"Not particularly."

"You can take it from me: he's a great man. I've only one reproach to make, and that is that he works too hard. At the rate he's going he'll wear himself out. Sometimes you can see it's telling on him. His nerves seem on edge."

"Lately?"

"From time to time . . . You see how he only let me take over your case when he was sure your wound had healed properly. And yours wasn't a very serious case. Most surgeons would have passed it on to their assistants from day one . . ."

"Is he very much liked by his colleagues?"

"They all admire him."

"I asked if they liked him."

"Yes . . . I think so . . . There's no reason why they shouldn't."

All the same, the tone had changed. Admiration was not the same thing as affection, and the assistant's voice showed it.

"Have you often been to his house?"

"Never. But I see him every day in the hospital."

"So you don't know his family? . . ."

The wound had been examined and the bandages were being replaced—Maigret knew the routine by heart now. The blinds were down, shutting out the sun, but every sound that was made in the place du Marché floated into the room.

"He has a beautiful sister-in-law."

The young medico went on bandaging, pretending not to have heard.

"He goes to Bordeaux now and again, I suppose?"

"He's called there sometimes. If he liked, he'd be called much farther afield than that. To Nice, Paris, and even abroad."

"Really? But he is still quite young."

"In a surgeon that's an asset. A lot of people don't like to have the older men operating on them."

That was all. The job was finished. The assistant washed his hands, couldn't find a towel, and stammered some reply to Madame Maigret's apology.

Here were some fresh features to be added to Dr. Rivaud's portrait. Among his colleagues he appeared to pass for a really remarkable surgeon. A man of boundless energy.

Was he ambitious? In the ordinary way one would have taken it for granted. Yet, if he was, why did he bury himself in a place like Bergerac?

"I can't make head or tail of it: can you?" said Madame Maigret as soon as they were alone.

"Put up the blind, will you? . . . One thing's certain anyhow. He must be a real doctor. It's not so difficult to impose upon patients in general practice, but he works in a hospital with colleagues and assistants . . ."

"But if the universities say he isn't qualified . . . ?"

"One thing at a time . . . For the moment I'm thinking of Leduc, and wondering how he's going to tackle Madame Beausoleil. She may prove rather a handful . . . Didn't you hear a train just now? If it's from Bordeaux, there's a chance of their showing up at any moment."

"What do you expect Madame Beausoleil to tell you?"

"You'll see . . . Throw me the matches, will you?"

He was very much better. His temperature was rarely over ninety-nine and the stiffness in his right arm had practically disappeared. The most encouraging sign of all was his inability to keep still in bed. Every minute he was fidgeting, stretching, turning over, or re-arranging his pillows.

"I think you ought to ring up a few people."

"Who?"

"I want to know the whereabouts of the chief people I'm interested in. Begin with the prosecutor. And as soon as you hear his voice, hang up."

It was done. Madame Maigret did the talking while he stared out onto the place du Marché, puffing away at his pipe.

"He's at home."

"Now the hospital. Ask for Rivaud."

They heard his voice answering: so that disposed of him.

"And now for his house.

"If Françoise answers, ask for Madame Rivaud. And if Madame Rivaud answers, ask for Françoise."

It was the elder sister who answered. She said Françoise was out, but could she take a message?

Maigret made a sign that meant:

"Hang up."

So there were three people who'd spend half the morning wondering who had rung them up.

Five minutes later the hotel omnibus came from the station, depositing three travelers and their luggage at the entrance below. Then a postman passed on a bicycle with the mailbag over his shoulder.

And finally the hooting of the well-known horn, followed by the Ford. Maigret could see there was somebody beside Leduc, and he thought there was a third person sitting behind.

He wasn't wrong. Leduc emerged first, looking anxiously round him, poor man: as though afraid he was making a fool of himself. Then he helped out his front-seat passenger, a stout lady who almost fell into his arms.

Meanwhile a girl had already leapt out from the back. Instinctively she looked up, to throw a venomous look in the direction of Maigret's window.

It was Françoise, dressed in a smartly tailored suit of tender green.

———

"May I stay?" asked Madame Maigret.

"Why not? . . . Open the door for them. Here they are."

A noise—one might almost say a row—approaching from the staircase. Heavy breathing from the stout lady, who came into the room mopping her brow.

"Where's this notary who isn't a notary?"

The voice was certainly vulgar. And not only the voice. She might have been hardly more than forty-five. In any case, she had not yet renounced her claims to beauty, for she was made up like any actress.

A fair woman, abundant in bosom—and elsewhere. Her lips were full and lacking in firmness.

Looking at her, Maigret's first impression was that he had already seen her. Of course he had—over and over again! For she was the very embodiment of a type he knew well, a type that was now becoming rare— the old-time *chanteuse de café-concert*. A heart-shaped mouth. A narrow waist. A saucy, challenging eye. And those milk-white shoulders, disclosed to the maximum. That little swing and swagger in the walk, and that way of looking at you as though across the footlights.

"Madame Beausoleil?" asked Maigret gallantly. "Please take a chair . . . And you too, mademoiselle . . ."

Françoise did not accept the invitation. Her nerves were as taut as a harp string.

"I warn you I shall complain," she said. "It's un-heard of . . ."

Leduc remained by the door, standing so piteously that it was easy to see things hadn't gone any too smoothly.

"Calm yourself, mademoiselle. And forgive me for having wanted to see your mother."

'Who said she was my mother?"

Madame Beausoleil was quite out of her depth. Be-wildered, she looked from Françoise, tense with fury, to the placid-faced invalid in bed.

"I took it for granted," said the latter. "The fact that you went to see her at the station . . ."

"Mademoiselle wanted to stop her mother coming," sighed Leduc, staring at the carpet.

"Oh! And what did you do?"

It was Françoise who answered:

"He threatened us. He even said something about a

warrant as if we were thieves. If he's got a warrant, let him show it. Otherwise . . ."

Her hand was stretched toward the telephone. There was not much doubt about it: Leduc had somewhat overstepped his rights. And he wasn't proud of it at all.

"I had to say something," he muttered. "They were on the point of making a scene."

"One moment, mademoiselle," asked Maigret. "Who are you going to ring up?"

"The prosecutor."

"Sit down . . . Mind you, you're quite free to telephone if you want to, but perhaps it would be better for everybody if you weren't in too much of a hurry."

"*Maman,* I forbid you to answer."

"I can't understand a word of this. What I'd like to know is: are you a notary or a policeman?"

"A policeman."

She smiled, as much as to say:

"In that case . . ."

It wasn't hard to guess she'd had dealings with the police before, and that she preserved a respect, or at least a fear, of that institution.

"But I can't see why . . . why I . . ."

"You have nothing to fear, madame. You'll understand in a moment. I've merely a few questions to ask you."

"Then there's no legacy?"

"I don't know that yet."

"It's disgusting," snarled Françoise. "Don't answer, *maman*."

She couldn't keep still. She had sat down after all, but was now on her feet again. With her fingernails she was fraying the edge of her handkerchief, throwing a baneful glance at Leduc from time to time.

"I take it that you're an *artiste lyrique* by profession?"

He knew very well that those two little words would go straight to her heart.

"Yes, monsieur. I sang at the Olympia at the time of . . ."

"I seem to remember your name . . . Beausoleil . . . Yvonne isn't it?"

"Joséphine Beausoleil . . . But the doctors recommended a warmer climate, and I went on tour in Italy. Turkey, Syria, and Egypt . . ."

At the time of the *cafés-chantants*. He could easily picture her on one of the little stages they had in those resorts that had been so fashionable in Paris and elsewhere, frequented by all the swells and the officers from the town . . . And after singing her song she would come down from the stage, and go round the tables carrying a tray, finally joining the company at one of them and drinking champagne . . .

"You fetched up in Algiers?"

"Yes. I'd had my first daughter in Cairo."

Françoise looked as though at any moment she might go into a fit of hysterics or throw herself at Maigret and scratch his eyes out.

"Of unknown father?"

"Nothing of the kind! I knew him very well. An English officer attached to the . . ."

"While your second girl, Françoise, was perhaps born in Algiers?"

"Yes. And that was the end of my theatrical career . . . I was ill for quite a long time, and though I got over it, I never recovered my voice."

"So then?"

"Her father looked after me, right up to the day he was recalled to France . . . You see, he was in the customs . . ."

It was all just what Maigret had imagined. Now he could piece together the lives of the mother and her two daughters in Algiers. Still good-looking, she had a number of male friends. The two girls were growing up . . . Wouldn't they naturally follow their mother's career?

"I wanted them to be dancers. That's a much less thankless job than singing. Particularly abroad. Germaine had begun to take lessons with an old friend of mine who had settled out there . . ."

"But she fell ill?"

"Did she tell you that? . . . As a matter of fact, she'd never been very strong. That's what comes of traveling so much when you're tiny. At least I always put it down to that. You see, I'd never leave her with anybody else. I had a little hammock for her, and I used to sling it between the luggage racks . . ."

A good soul, obviously. She was quite at her ease

now, and she couldn't understand why Françoise
should have made such a fuss. Why shouldn't she come
and see Maigret? A very nicely spoken man, he was. He
came straight to the point, in a language she could understand. And he didn't hurt her feelings.

She was an artiste. She'd traveled. She'd had affairs.
She'd had two children . . . But wasn't that all in the
natural order of things?

"Was it chest trouble?"

"No. In her head. She was always complaining of
headaches . . . And then one day she caught meningitis
and had to be rushed off to the hospital."

A pause. So far it had just gushed out of its own accord, but Joséphine Beausoleil had now come to the
critical point. She seemed to know she was on dangerous ground, for she looked inquiringly at Françoise,
wondering what she ought to say next.

"The inspector has no right to question you, *maman*.
Don't answer another word."

That was easy to say. But she, Joséphine Beausoleil,
knew very well that it was a risky business rubbing the
police up the wrong way. She didn't want to offend
anybody.

Leduc had quite recovered his self-respect and was
now throwing looks at Maigret that said:

"We're making headway."

"Listen, madame! . . . You're quite at liberty to
speak or not—just as you think fit. You've every right to

refuse. But it doesn't alter the fact that you can be made to speak sooner or later . . . somewhere or other . . . in the assize court, for instance . . ."

"But I haven't done anything."

"Exactly. And that's why, in my opinion, the wisest course would be to be perfectly frank . . . As for you, Mademoiselle Françoise . . ."

But Françoise wasn't listening. She had picked up the telephone receiver and was speaking breathlessly. Her voice was anxious, feverish, and she kept on glancing furtively at Leduc as though she expected him to snatch the instrument out of her hand.

"Hallo! . . . He's going round the wards? . . . Never mind. Tell him he must come at once. There's not a minute to lose. To the Hôtel d' Angleterre . . . Say it's from Mademoiselle Françoise . . . Yes. He'll understand . . ."

She listened a moment longer, then put the receiver down and turned a look of defiance on Maigret.

"He's coming . . . Don't say anything, *maman*."

She was trembling. Beads of sweat rolled down her forehead and wetted her chestnut hair at the temples.

"You see, inspector . . ." began Madame Beausoleil. "What can I do?"

Without answering her, Maigret turned to the daughter.

"Mademoiselle Françoise, please take note of the fact that I made no attempt to stop you telephoning. And I shan't ask your mother any more questions. But let me give you a word of advice. Since you've asked Dr. Rivaud to come, ask the prosecutor too. You'll find him at his house."

She tried to guess his thoughts. She hesitated. But in the end she snatched up the receiver again.

"Hallo! . . . 167, please."

"Here! Leduc!"

And Maigret whispered a few words into his ear.

Leduc seemed surprised and embarrassed.

"Do you think . . . ?" he began. But he broke off, and half a minute later they could hear him cranking the Ford.

"Hallo! . . . It's Françoise speaking . . . Yes . . . I'm speaking from the Hôtel d' Angleterre—the inspector's room. My mother's here . . . Yes, the inspector wants you to come . . . No . . . No! . . . No, I assure you . . ."

This torrent of "nos" burst out of her in a flood of anguish.

"NO! . . . I tell you . . ."

She stood by the bedside table, tense, panting.

Maigret smiled at her as he lit his pipe, while Madame Beausoleil repowdered her face.

10

THE NOTE

The silence seemed to have lasted an age when all at once Françoise frowned. She was looking out of the window with acute anxiety on her face. Then suddenly she turned her head away.

It was Madame Rivaud crossing the place du Marché, coming toward the hotel. Was it an optical illusion? Or was it that the gravity of the moment made everything seem dramatic? Even at that distance she seemed like a person in a play. She walked as though she was being driven on by some invisible force that had completely taken hold of her.

As she came closer it could be seen that her face was pale and her hair disheveled. Her overcoat was unbuttoned.

"Here's Germaine," said Madame Beausoleil at last. "Someone must have told her I was here."

Madame Maigret went instinctively to open the door. When Madame Rivaud entered, it was written all over her that she was living through a tragic moment.

She made, nevertheless, a great effort to control herself. She even managed to smile. But there was a wild, lost look in her eyes, and from time to time her features twitched involuntarily.

"Excuse me, inspector . . . But I heard my mother and sister were here . . ."

"Who told you?"

"Who . . . ?" she repeated, trembling.

What a contrast they presented—those two sisters. Germaine was obviously the one who had to make the sacrifices, who had to take a backseat. She had never quite outgrown her plebeian origin, and so was entitled to less consideration than Françoise. Even her mother looked critically at her.

"What! Do you mean you don't know?"

"It was someone I met."

"You haven't seen your husband?"

"No . . . Really . . . I swear I haven't."

Maigret, puzzled, looked in turn at the three women, then out onto the place du Marché, where there was no sign of either Rivaud or Leduc. What did that mean? Leduc had been dispatched to keep an eye on the doctor in case the latter made off instead of coming to the hotel. He looked at Madame Rivaud's dusty shoes—she must have been running on the road. Then he studied her sister's drawn features. He had forgotten his wife's presence, but suddenly she bent over him, saying:

"Give me that pipe. You've had quite enough."

He was about to protest, but as he opened his mouth he noticed a little piece of paper that she had dropped on the bed. On it was scribbled:

*Madame Rivaud has just passed a note to
Françoise, who is holding it in her left hand.*

The sunshine outside. All the noises of the town blend-
ing into a chant that Maigret knew by heart. Madame
Beausoleil waited, sitting bolt upright in her chair, like
a woman who at any rate knows how to hold herself
properly. Madame Rivaud, on the other hand, had quite
lost countenance. She had no more dignity than a guilty
schoolgirl.

"Mademoiselle Françoise . . ." began Maigret.

She shook from head to foot. For a second she looked
straight into Maigret's eyes. A hard, intelligent look.
For all her nervousness she was not one to lose her head.

"Mademoiselle Françoise, would you mind coming
over here?"

Good old Madame Maigret! Did she guess what was
coming! Anyhow she made a movement toward the door.
But she was not quick enough. Françoise made a dash for
it, rushed out, along the passage, and down the stairs.

"What's the matter with her?" asked Joséphine
Beausoleil, quite concerned.

Maigret did not move. He couldn't. Nor could he
very well send his wife off in pursuit. He merely turned
to Madame Rivaud and asked:

"When did your husband give you that note?"

"What note?"

Maigret took pity on her. Besides, what was the
good of insisting? He turned to his wife.

"Go and look out of one of the rear windows of the hotel."

The prosecutor chose the moment to make his entry. He came in stiffly. And, to cover his uneasiness no doubt, his expression was severe and even threatening.

"I received a telephone message asking me to . . ."

"Sit down, Monsieur Duhourceau."

"But . . . the person who telephoned . . ."

"Françoise has just escaped. Perhaps she'll be caught. But, on the other hand, perhaps not . . . Do sit down, please. You know Madame Beausoleil, I think . . ."

"I? . . . Nothing of the sort!"

He tried to fathom Maigret's look. For the latter seemed to be talking for the sake of talking, while really thinking of other things; or rather he seemed with his mind's eye to be watching some scene that was hidden from the rest of them. He looked out of the window, listened, then stared at Madame Rivaud.

Suddenly there were noises. Perhaps a shot had been fired but anyhow there was a general hustle and scurry. Running steps on the stairs. Doors slamming. People calling.

"What's up? . . . Who is it? . . ."

More shouts. Noise of something being broken. Steps rushing in pursuit on the floor above. A window was smashed, the shards falling onto the pavement below.

Madame Maigret burst into the room, locking the door behind her.

"I think Leduc's got them," she panted.

"Leduc?" asked the prosecutor suspiciously.

"The doctor's car was in the lane behind. He was sitting in it, waiting for somebody. Françoise ran up to it and was just getting in when Leduc drove up in the Ford. I almost shouted to him to be quick, for he simply sat there and looked at them. But he had his own idea. He quietly pulled out a revolver and punctured one of the tires . . .

"The other two didn't know what to do. The doctor looked wildly round him, first this way, then that . . . But when he saw Leduc coming toward him, still holding his revolver, he jumped out, caught Françoise by the arm, and dashed into the hotel, dragging her after him . . .

"Leduc's on their heels . . . They're upstairs."

———————

"I should be grateful for some explanation," snapped the prosecutor, though he was pale as death.

"It's quite simple," answered Maigret. "By means of a little advertisement I got Madame Beausoleil to come and see me. But she wasn't the only one to see it in the paper, and Dr. Rivaud, who didn't wish the interview to take place, sent Françoise to the station to intercept her . . .

"However, I had foreseen that maneuver and posted Leduc at the station too. Instead of bringing one woman he brought both of them here.

"You'll see how it all links up . . . Françoise, seeing things were going from bad to worse, rang up Rivaud and told him to come at once.

"I sent Leduc to keep track of Rivaud, but he must have arrived at the hospital too late. Rivaud had gone. He drove home, wrote a note for Françoise and told Madame Rivaud to slip it to her. Then he drove round to the lane at the back . . . Do you see? . . . That's where Françoise was to join him . . .

"A minute more and they might have made it. But in the meantime Leduc turns up in his Ford, guesses there's something fishy going on, and shoots out a tire, and . . ."

The shindy on the floor above was louder than ever. Then suddenly it ceased. Dead silence. A silence so impressive that in the room below no one moved an eyelid.

Leduc's voice now. Giving orders. But it was impossible to make out what he said . . . Then more noise: a dull bang, then another, then another—finally, the noise of a door being broken down.

Silence again, and this time it was positively painful. What did it mean? Why was no one moving, upstairs?

At last there were steps on the floor above. A man's steps, slow and ponderous.

Madame Rivaud stood riveted where she was, wide-eyed, breathless. The prosecutor yanked at his mustache. Joséphine Beausoleil was on the verge of tears.

"They must be dead," said Maigret gravely, looking at the ceiling.

"What? . . . What do you mean? . . ."

Madame Rivaud was jolted out of her stillness. She darted forward toward the bed, her panic-stricken eyes staring into Maigret's.

"It's not true . . . It can't be . . . Say it isn't true . . ."

The steps came down the stairs. The door opened. It was Leduc who entered. His tie was askew, and a lock of hair had fallen over his forehead.

"Dead?"

"Both of them."

He raised an arm to bar the door as Madame Rivaud ran toward it.

"Not yet."

"It isn't true. I know it isn't . . . Let me see them," she panted.

Madame Beausoleil was trying desperately to take it in. Monsieur Duhourceau fixed his eyes on the carpet. Perhaps at bottom he was the most astonished and upset of any of them.

"How? . . . Both of them? . . ." he at last managed to stammer, looking up at Leduc.

"We dashed upstairs after them, but they had time to slip into one of the rooms and lock the door behind them. It was too solid for me . . . I sent for the landlord, who is a big, strong chap . . . I was able to see them through the keyhole."

Madame Rivaud listened avidly. She seemed almost out of her mind. So much so that Leduc shot an inquiring look at Maigret to know if he ought to go on.

Why not? Just as well get it over. It would all come out before long. Maigret nodded.

"They were in each other's arms. She was holding on to him frantically. I could hear her say:

"'I won't . . . No. It's impossible . . . I'd rather . . .'

"And it was she who dragged the revolver out of his pocket.

"'Both of us . . .' she said. 'Shoot . . . Shoot as you kiss me! . . .'

"I couldn't see anymore, as we started to hack the door down."

He wiped his forehead. You could see even through his trouser legs that his knees were shaking.

"It took us half a minute to get it down, and of course we were too late. Rivaud was already dead when I bent over him. The girl's eyes seemed to be looking at me, but I thought it was the same with her . . . I thought it was all over. And then suddenly, when I least expected it . . ."

"What was it?" asked the prosecutor, with something like a sob in his voice.

"She smiled . . . She smiled at me . . . I had the door put across the doorway and gave orders nobody was to go in. They're telephoning to the hospital and the police."

For all her efforts, Madame Beausoleil was unable to take it in. She stared vacantly at Leduc. Then, turning to Maigret, she asked in a dreamy voice:

"What's he saying?"

The door opened and the landlord came in. His face was redder than ever, and as he spoke he breathed a gust of alcohol into the air. He had been downstairs and, to pull himself together, had swilled down a stiff drink at the bar. The shoulder of his white coat was dirty and a seam had burst.

"A doctor's arrived. Shall I show him up?"

"I'll go," said Leduc reluctantly.

"Monsieur le procureur?" went on the landlord. "I didn't know you were here. I suppose you've heard? . . . It's a sight I shall never forget. Enough to make your heart bleed. Such a fine-looking couple . . . To see them lying there holding each other . . ."

"That'll do," said Maigret. "Leave us."

"Ought I to shut the hotel? The crowd's gathering thick and fast. When I rang up the police, the inspector wasn't there, but they're sending some men round . . ."

As soon as he had gone, Maigret looked round for Germaine Rivaud. He found her stretched full-length on Madame Maigret's bed, with her head buried in the pillow. There were no tears, no sobs. Nothing but long, painful groans, as might have come from a wounded animal.

Madame Beausoleil, who had at last grasped the situation, dried her eyes and in a firm decisive voice asked:

"May I go and see them?"

"Presently. The doctor's there now."

Madame Maigret hovered round Germaine. But

what help or consolation could she offer? The prosecutor mumbled:

"I told you . . ."

Through the window came the half-subdued murmur of an expectant crowd. Two policemen had arrived and were elbowing their way through, while the onlookers complained resentfully of their roughness.

Maigret filled himself a pipe. At the same time he looked thoughtfully out of the window at the little grocer's shop over the way, all of whose customers he now knew by sight.

"You left the child at Bordeaux, Madame Beausoleil?"

She looked inquiringly at the prosecutor, but she got no help from him.

"Yes . . . I . . ."

"About three years old, I suppose?"

"Two."

"A boy?"

"A little girl . . . But . . ."

"Her mother was Françoise, wasn't she?"

But Monsieur Duhourceau intervened. Rising from his chair, he began:

"Really, inspector . . . I must ask you . . ."

"You're quite right. Perhaps you'd like to call on me another time. Or rather, the first day I'm allowed out, I'll pay you a visit myself."

The prosecutor was obviously relieved.

"By that time," went on Maigret, "it will all be cleared

up . . . It is now, for that matter, or practically so. And no doubt your place is upstairs, seeing to the official side of things."

Monsieur Duhourceau made off precipitately, without thinking of saying good-bye. He fled, in fact, like a schoolboy who has suddenly been let off a punishment.

With his departure the atmosphere of the room became at once more intimate. Germaine was still groaning, while Madame Maigret vainly tried to soothe her by putting cold compresses on her forehead. But Germaine pushed them away, letting the water trickle down onto the pillow.

Madame Beausoleil sat down again with a sigh.

"Whoever would have thought . . . ?"

A good woman at heart. In her way a thoroughly moral one. That is, if mortality is living according to your lights. Was it her fault if her lights were not so steady as some people's?

Big round tears began to well up from her lined middle-aged eyes and run down her cheeks, washing away the makeup.

"She was your favorite, wasn't she?"

Germaine's presence didn't worry her at all, though it's only fair to add that the latter wasn't listening.

"Of course. She had the looks. And such style too. Far more intelligent than her sister. Oh, it wasn't Germaine's fault. You can't blame her, as she was ill such a lot, and couldn't help being backward . . . When the doctor married her, Françoise was too young—barely thirteen. But, believe me or not, I had an idea even then that there'd be trouble later . . . And you see what's happened . . ."

"What was Rivaud's name in Algiers?"

"Dr. Meyer . . . I suppose there's no use trying to hide it any longer. Considering what you've found out already, you're bound to know it all in the end."

"This man Samuel was his father?"

"Yes."

"And he arranged his father's escape from the hospital in Algiers?"

"That's right. In fact, that's how things started with Germaine. There were only three of them in that wing of the hospital: Germaine, Samuel, as he was called, and another. One night Rivaud set the place on fire, and it was this third person who was left in the flames and afterward given out to be Samuel. It sounds terrible, but the doctor always swore the man was dead already. I think he was telling the truth. After all, he wasn't a bad man. You could tell that from the way he treated his father. He could have washed his hands of him after the way he'd behaved . . ."

"So that's how it was done . . . The other man was entered in the register of death as Samuel Meyer . . . And then the doctor married Germaine, and brought the three of you to France?"

"Not at once. We were quite a time in Spain waiting for his papers."

"And Samuel?"

"He was shipped off to America and told never to come back. The trial seemed to have unhinged him. He was already a bit queer."

"Finally, when your son-in-law received his papers in the name of Rivaud, he came here with his wife and sister-in-law. And you?"

"He gave me an allowance and set me up in Bordeaux . . . I should have preferred Marseilles or Nice—particularly Nice—but he wanted to keep an eye on me . . . Goodness! How he worked! Whatever they say about him, nobody can deny he was a good doctor. And I feel sure he wouldn't have done *that* to a patient, not even for his own father . . ."

To shut out the hubbub of the crowd, Maigret had had the windows shut. The room was getting hot and stuffy and full of pipe smoke.

Germaine was still wailing like a child.

"She's been worse than before," her mother explained, "since the operation on her head. And she was always rather gloomy . . . You see, having spent so much of her life in bed . . . But, as I said, she was worse afterward. She would cry for nothing at all. And scared of the least thing . . ."

Bergerac had accepted the newcomers without a suspicion. A quiet little town where a dangerous, hectic past could gradually be forgotten.

Nobody guessed a thing. They gossiped about "the doctor's house," "the doctor's car," "the doctor's wife," "the doctor's sister-in-law." And all they saw was a cosy little villa in English cottage style; a handsome, stylish car; a dashing lively young sister; a somewhat weary-looking wife.

Meanwhile, in a little flat in Bordeaux, Joséphine Beausoleil was peacefully winding up her restless life. She who had known so much care for the morrow, who had been dependent on the whims of so many men, could at last adopt the ways and habits of a woman of private, even if modest, means.

No doubt she was respected in her neighborhood. She could lead a regular life and pay her bills regularly. And when, from time to time, her daughters came to see her, there was always the same satisfaction in seeing them drive up in that handsome, stylish car.

She was crying again now, and blowing her nose into an inadequate handkerchief that was almost all lace.

"If only you'd known Françoise . . . For instance, when she came to have the baby . . . Oh, there's no harm in speaking in front of Germaine. She knows all about it . . ."

Madame Maigret listened, horrified by this unbelievable world that was being unfolded before her.

Cars had arrived outside. They brought the police pathologist and the examining magistrate and his clerk. The local inspector too, who had been run to earth in the marketplace of a neighboring village where he was busy buying some rabbits.

There was a knock on the door and Leduc cautiously

looked in, throwing an inquiring glance at Maigret to know if he was intruding.

"Later on, old chap . . . If you don't mind . . ."

Maigret did not want anything to disturb an atmosphere that encouraged Madame Beausoleil to be so confiding. Leduc nevertheless came up to the bed to whisper:

"If they want to see the bodies before they're moved . . ."

"No. There's no point in it."

Indeed, what good could it do? Even Madame Beausoleil, who had wanted to see them before, was now only waiting for Leduc's departure to resume her confidences. She felt at ease with the big man who was lying in bed and who looked at her good-naturedly, comprehendingly.

Yes, he understood. He never looked surprised. Never asked stupid questions.

"You were talking of Françoise . . ."

"Oh, yes . . . Well, when the child was born . . . But perhaps you don't know . . ."

"I know."

"Who told you?"

"Monsieur Duhourceau was there, wasn't he?"

"Yes. And I've never seen a man so jumpy and so miserable. He said it was a crime to bring children into the world, as there was no knowing if it wouldn't kill the mother . . . He could hear her groaning from the other room . . . Though I did what I could for him—I kept on filling up his glass . . ."

"You've quite a big flat?"

"Three rooms."

"You had a midwife?"

"Yes . . . Rivaud said he couldn't manage all alone."

"You live near the harbor?"

"Near the bridge, in a little street where . . ."

Again a scene that Maigret could picture almost as well as if it had been from memory. But at the same time there was another—the one that was being enacted at that very moment overhead.

Rivaud and Françoise. The doctor and the undertakers dragging the couple apart. The prosecutor was no doubt whiter than those printed forms that the examining magistrate's clerk would be filling up with a shaking hand . . .

And the police inspector who an hour before had been thinking of nothing but rabbits . . .

"When Monsieur Duhourceau heard he'd got a daughter he actually cried. Yes, he did, as true as I'm here, and he put his head on my shoulder . . . I thought he was going to be taken really bad . . . I didn't want to let him go into the room, because . . . After all . . ."

She stopped, suddenly on her guard, and shot a mistrustful glance at Maigret.

"I'm only a poor woman that's done the best I could . . . It's a shame to take advantage of it to make me say more than I . . ."

Germaine Rivaud had stopped moaning. Sitting on the edge of the bed, she stared with wide eyes straight in front of her.

The worst moment of all had come. They were carrying the bodies down on stretchers . . . treading heavily, carefully on the stairs . . . step-by-step . . .

And someone calling out:

"Steady now! Look out!"

A little later someone knocked on the door. It was Leduc, and he too had had a drink to stiffen himself up.

"It's all over."

Below, the ambulance drove off . . .

11

THE FATHER

"What name shall I say?"

"Inspector Maigret."

The latter smiled at nothing in particular—merely because it felt so good to be on his feet again and walking about like anybody else. He was even rather proud of it, like a child enjoying its first unaided steps.

All the same, he was none too steady on his legs, and when the manservant had gone to announce him he rather hastily dragged a chair toward him and sank into it, for he was conscious of a sweat breaking out on his forehead.

It was the manservant with the striped waistcoat. A man of extremely rustic features whose head was a trifle turned by the high position to which he had risen!

"Will you come this way, sir?" he said, reappearing. "*Monsieur le procureur* will see you in a moment."

The manservant had probably no idea what a labor it could be to climb a flight of stairs! Maigret knew all about it before he reached the first floor. He was hot all over. He leaned on to the banisters, counting the steps.

Eight more . . .

"This way, please. If you wouldn't mind waiting a moment . . ."

The house was just as Maigret had imagined it. And there he was, in the study with the tall windows that his mind had so often dwelt on.

The white ceiling was divided by heavy, varnished oak beams. An immense fireplace. And all those bookcases. They almost covered the walls.

There was no one there. No steps could be heard in the house, as all the floors were thickly carpeted. Maigret was longing to sit down. Instead of doing so, however, he walked over to one of the bookcases, the lower half of which was enclosed by metal-grilled doors behind which hung green curtains, hiding the shelves from view.

It was with some difficulty that he thrust one of his thick fingers through the latticework to draw aside one of the curtains. When he did so, all he discovered was empty shelves.

Turning round, he found Monsieur Duhourceau watching him.

"I've been expecting you for the last two days . . . I must confess . . ."

He looked as if he had lost ten kilos. His cheeks sagged, and the lines at the corners of his mouth were twice as deep as they had been.

"Won't you sit down, inspector?"

The prosecutor was ill at ease. He couldn't look

Maigret in the face. He sat down in his usual place in front of a desk laden with files and documents.

More than once he had treated Maigret with scant civility. More than once he had been openly hostile. He had, however, had plenty of time to regret it, and it seemed to Maigret most charitable to finish off quickly.

A man of sixty-five, all alone in that large house, practically alone in that town of Bergerac in which he was the highest officer of the law . . . In fact, all alone in life . . .

"I see you've burned your books."

No answer from Monsieur Duhourceau. Only a faint flush mounting to his haggard cheeks.

"And now let's get this case wound up. It's clear enough. I don't think there's room for any two opinions about it . . .

"To begin with, there's a certain Samuel Meyer, a commercial adventurer who's ready to put his hand to anything profitable, not excluding those branches of trade that are forbidden by law.

"At the same time he has social ambitions—not for himself but for his son. The latter studies medicine and becomes assistant to the great Dr. Martel. A brilliant future seems assured . . .

"Then the trouble begins.

"First act: two of Samuel's accomplices come to Algiers and threaten him. He dispatches them into the next world.

"Second act: Samuel is condemned to death. But his

son intervenes. Diagnoses meningitis or something of the kind. Has the old man removed to his own hospital and saves him with the help of a fire.

"Another man is buried in Samuel's place. Was he dead already? We'll never know.

"The young Meyer, who henceforth adopts the name Rivaud, is not one of those men who needs to bare his soul. He is strong, self-sufficient.

"And ambitious! A man of keen intelligence, who knows his own worth and wants to realize it at whatever cost.

"Just one chink in the armor: he falls vaguely in love with a patient and marries her, only to realize, some time later, how colorless she is."

The prosecutor sat still. This part of the story was of no great interest, but he was listening for the sequel with keen apprehension.

"The second act finishes with Samuel in America and Madame Beausoleil in Bordeaux, while Dr. Rivaud with his wife and sister-in-law have settled down in Bergerac . . .

"And of course the inevitable happens. This young girl he has under his roof begins to intrigue him, gets under his skin, and finally seduces him.

"And now for the third act. By some means or other—I have no idea how—the public prosecutor of Bergerac begins to find out something of Rivaud's past . . . Is that correct?"

Monsieur Duhourceau replied without hesitation:

"Absolutely correct."

"Then his mouth must be kept shut . . . Rivaud knows what others know—that the prosecutor has a relatively harmless failing, that he collects 'books for connoisseurs.' He knows that's a pastime of lonely bachelors who find stamp collecting rather tame.

"Rivaud takes advantage of this. He introduces his sister-in-law to you as a model secretary. She is to help you in classifying certain papers. And gradually she entices you into paying her attention.

"But that's not enough. Rivaud doesn't want to start wandering again. He's getting on splendidly. His name's beginning to be known, and he's determined not to change it.

"A temporary affair with Françoise is not enough. He must have a stronger hold over you than that. She is going to have a baby. She must convince you that the baby will be yours.

"Again she succeeds. And now they hold you in a vice. You won't be talking now. For you too have a secret that must not come to light—a secret birth in Joséphine Beausoleil's flat in Bordeaux, and secret visits thenceforward, when you go to see the child you take to be yours."

Maigret had the delicacy not to look at Monsieur Duhourceau as he spoke.

"You see, Rivaud was, above all, ambitious. He knew himself to be abler than other men, and nothing was going to stop him getting to the top. He was ready to go to any lengths to keep his buried past underground. He really loved Françoise, he loved her dearly—but not so much as he loved his career. For that, he was ready to push her, once at any rate, into your arms . . . Might I ask you one question? Was it once?"

"Only once."

"Then she edged away?"

"On various pretexts . . . She thought it shameful . . ."

"No, no! She loved Rivaud—as much as he did her. Perhaps more. And it was only to save him . . ."

Maigret still kept his eyes turned away from the man who sat listening at his desk. He stared into the open fireplace, where three logs were blazing.

"You are convinced the child is yours. From now on, you'll keep your mouth shut. You are invited to the villa. You visit your daughter in Bordeaux.

"Meanwhile, in America, our Samuel—the Samuel of Poland and Algiers—has gone completely mad. He attacked two women somewhere near Chicago. In each case, after strangling them, he stuck a needle through the heart. I found this out from police records.

"He wasn't caught, and fleeing the country, he came to France, finally turning up in Bergerac practically penniless. Rivaud gave him money and told him to clear out. He did so, but in another fit of madness he left a corpse behind him.

"Exactly the same. First strangulation, then the needle. It was in the woods by Moulin-Neuf. He was on his way to the station . . . I don't know whether you suspected the truth."

"No, I can swear to that . . . Not then."

"He came back, and the same thing happened . . . He came a third time but this time failed. Each time Rivaud bribed him to go away. What else could he do? He couldn't put him in an asylum, still less have him arrested."

"I told him that this had to end."

"Yes, and he made arrangements accordingly. Old Samuel rang him up. He told him to jump out of the train just before the station."

The prosecutor was pale as death. He couldn't have uttered a word to save his life.

"And that's all. Rivaud killed him. Nothing was to stand between him and the future for which he was destined. Not even his wife—one day or other he'd have shoved her off too into a better world. For he loved Françoise—the girl who had given him a daughter, that daughter who . . ."

"Enough!"

And Maigret got up simply, as though this had been any other sort of visit.

"That's all, *monsieur le procureur*."

"But . . ."

"They were a pair—those two. The one as spirited as the other. Not the sort to knuckle under. He had the woman he needed. Françoise, who was willing to suffer your embrace for his sake . . ."

He was talking to a poor sunken old man, too numb to react.

"And now they're dead. Those who are left will give no trouble. Madame Rivaud is neither brilliant nor dangerous—nor is she guilty of anything. She'll have enough to live on. She'll join her mother in Bordeaux or elsewhere . . . They won't talk."

Maigret picked up his hat from a chair.

"As for me, I must be getting back to Paris. I've been away long enough."

He walked up to the desk.

"Good-bye, *monsieur le procureur*."

The latter pounced upon the outstretched hand with such gratitude that Maigret feared a flood of thanks. To stave them off he hastily added:

"No hard feelings!"

A few moments later the manservant with the striped waistcoat was showing him out. He slowly crossed the sunlit marketplace and dragged himself rather laboriously back to the Hôtel d' Angleterre, where he said to the proprietor:

"We'll have truffles and foie gras for lunch, if you please. And you can serve the bill with it. We're leaving."

FOR THE BEST IN PAPERBACKS, LOOK FOR THE

In every corner of the world, on every subject under the sun, Penguin represents quality and variety—the very best in publishing today.

For complete information about books available from Penguin—including Penguin Classics and Puffins—and how to order them, write to us at the appropriate address below. Please note that for copyright reasons the selection of books varies from country to country.

In the United States: Please write to *Penguin Group (USA), P.O. Box 12289 Dept. B, Newark, New Jersey 07101-5289* or call 1-800-788-6262.

In the United Kingdom: Please write to *Dept. EP, Penguin Books Ltd, Bath Road, Harmondsworth, West Drayton, Middlesex UB7 0DA.*

In Canada: Please write to *Penguin Books Canada Ltd, 90 Eglinton Avenue East, Suite 700, Toronto, Ontario M4P 2Y3.*

In Australia: Please write to *Penguin Books Australia Ltd, P.O. Box 257, Ringwood, Victoria 3134.*

In New Zealand: Please write to *Penguin Books (NZ) Ltd, Private Bag 102902, North Shore Mail Centre, Auckland 10.*

In India: Please write to *Penguin Books India Pvt Ltd, 11 Panchsheel Shopping Centre, Panchsheel Park, New Delhi 110 017.*

In the Netherlands: Please write to *Penguin Books Netherlands bv, Postbus 3507, NL-1001 AH Amsterdam.*

In Germany: Please write to *Penguin Books Deutschland GmbH, Metzlerstrasse 26, 60594 Frankfurt am Main.*

In Spain: Please write to *Penguin Books S. A., Bravo Murillo 19, 1° B, 28015 Madrid.*

In Italy: Please write to *Penguin Italia s.r.l., Via Benedetto Croce 2, 20094 Corsico, Milano.*

In France: Please write to *Penguin France, Le Carré Wilson, 62 rue Benjamin Baillaud, 31500 Toulouse.*

In Japan: Please write to *Penguin Books Japan Ltd, Kaneko Building, 2-3-25 Koraku, Bunkyo-Ku, Tokyo 112.*

In South Africa: Please write to *Penguin Books South Africa (Pty) Ltd, Private Bag X14, Parkview, 2122 Johannesburg.*